Windsor and Eton Step by Step

Also by Christopher Turner

Windsor and Eton
Step by Step

CHRISTOPHER
TURNER

faber and faber

LONDON · BOSTON

First published in 1986 by
Faber and Faber Limited
3 Queen Square London WC1N 3AU

Photoset by Parker Typesetting Service, Leicester
Printed in Great Britain by
The Bath Press Ltd, Bath
All rights reserved

British Library Cataloguing in Publication Data
Turner, Christopher, *1934–*
Windsor and Eton Step by Step.
1. Windsor (Berkshire)—Description—
Guide-books   2. Eton (Berkshire)—
Description—Guide-books
I. Title
914.22'96   DA690.W757
ISBN 0-571-14529-9

Contents

Introduction

Windsor and Eton are two relatively small adjoining towns, the former possessing Europe's most important royal castle, and the latter Europe's best known college. Windsor Castle and Eton College are both open to the public, attracting between them several million visitors each year. Both may be reached quickly and easily from central London.

I was astonished, therefore, to discover that there was no pocket-size book available that provided a comprehensive guide to these tremendous attractions and the ancient and picturesque towns in which they stand.

Pictorial souvenirs, erudite volumes, a handful of pages in general tourist guides, these all existed in plenty, but none were of much practical help to the stranger suddenly confronted with a confusing array of stone walls and towers. It was time to remedy the situation.

Windsor and Eton Step by Step follows the pattern set by *London Step by Step* (voted 1985 Guide Book of the Year) and *Outer London Step by Step* which is being published simultaneously with this volume.

Windsor Castle is, in most cases, the prime reason for visiting the area and therefore forms the major part of this book. It is dealt with as if it were a medieval town, which it effectively is. On arrival the visitor is led, literally step by step, around each section of the castle, which is described exactly as it is reached. Windsor town, Eton College and Eton town are then explored in the same way.

Whether on a guided tour or a 'do-it-yourself' visit, this book will add immeasurably to your appreciation of these historic towns. You will know what is open and when, you won't have to have an advanced knowledge of English history and, above all, you won't get lost.

The development of Windsor

Following the surrender of London in 1066, William the Conqueror divided much of his invading army into relatively small garrisons which required protection from potential rebels. Fortifications were constructed initially in the form of a motte (central mound), surmounted by wooden buildings and enclosed by ditches and walls of earth reinforced with timber. The bailey (precinct within the outer walls) was generally divided into separately defended wards.

Windsor Castle was one of seven fortifications that surrounded London. Each was sited approximately twenty miles distant from its neighbour and from the Tower of London, so that Norman reinforcements were never more than one day's march away.

The site chosen for the fortification that became Windsor Castle was a prominent chalk escarpment overlooking the Thames, with extensive views of the surrounding countryside and steep easily defended slopes to its north, east and west. Due to the porous nature of the chalk, and the difficulty of raising sufficient water, the ditches here never became moats as they did, for example, at the Tower of London.

The castle was divided into Lower, Middle and Upper Wards which still retain their identity.

Windsor Castle gained its name from an ancient settlement nearby, Windlesora, now Old Windsor, where there was a modest residence belonging to the Saxon kings. No town of Windsor existed when the earliest fortification was constructed. Henry II strengthened the castle's defences by rebuilding the walls, central keep and royal apartments with stone. Henry III completed the work and constructed the first recorded chapel within the castle.

Edward III rebuilt most of the royal apartments and added more bastion towers. He also founded the Order of the Garter and adapted the existing chapel to accommodate its ceremonies. Edward IV commissioned the much larger St George's Chapel to take over the functions of the earlier building which was, however, retained as the Lady Chapel.

Henry VII adapted the old chapel (now the Albert Memorial Chapel) to provide a tomb house for himself and Henry VI, whom he venerated. Meanwhile, he continued with the construction of St George's Chapel, but work proceeded slowly and was not completed until the reign of his son, Henry VIII.

Charles II rebuilt most of the private royal apartments (now the State Apartments) but the interiors of only three of his rooms survived the early 19C remodelling by *Wyatville* for George IV.

New private apartments for the Royal Family were also created by *Wyatville* who, at the same time, doubled the height of the Round Tower.

Windsor Castle was the favourite residence of Queen Victoria and it became, until the death of her husband, Prince Albert, the social centre of the country. Most of the exterior of the castle, particularly its walls and bastion towers, owes its detailing to the restoration and rebuilding in the 'Romantic' style of the 19C.

The town of Windsor was created by, and evolved with, the castle, its primary function being to provide accommodation and services for the Court and visitors to the garrison. Windsor's tiny core, south of the castle, survives in the form of a network of narrow streets, lined by properties dating from the Tudor period.

With the coming of the railway in the nineteenth century, the town expanded rapidly but has never been allowed to encroach on the Great Park which covers almost five thousand acres.

The bridge across the Thames that for centuries has linked Windsor with Eton is now restricted to pedestrians only.

The development of Eton

Eton was an established riverside village before the college was founded to the north. Its High Street evolved following the route taken by 15C workmen transporting building materials from the river to the college.

Eton College is judged by many to be England's most prestigious public school. It was founded by Henry VI in 1440 as the King's College of Our Lady of Eton beside Windsor. The King, who was only twenty at the time, founded King's College, Cambridge, one year later, to facilitate the transition of Eton's scholars to university. Henry had recently seen, and been impressed by, Winchester College which, together with New College, Oxford, had been founded by William of Wykeham in a similar way.

A medieval college was not primarily a place of learning, but a religious foundation. At Eton, the King's foundation paid for a pilgrimage church served by secular (as opposed to monastic) priests, a school with accommodation for twenty-four boys from Eton town and an almshouse for twenty-four elderly men, also from the locality. A provost, appointed by the sovereign, and priest fellows were responsible for the college. In use by 1448 were the church, soon to be rebuilt on a grander scale as College Chapel, most of the cloister and an almshouse. A dining hall was completed shortly afterwards.

Henry VI was deposed in 1461 by Edward IV, who obtained a papal bull abolishing the college; all its property was seized. Eton College appeared to be doomed but the King relented, due, it is said, to the intervention of his mistress, Jane Shore, and the papal bull was reversed in 1470. However, Eton's funds were greatly reduced and much of its property was not returned. The almshouse was abandoned but the number of scholars increased to seventy. Although College Chapel was completed, in truncated form, at the expense of William Waynflete in 1482, its servants were greatly reduced in number.

By 1500, a new range, 'College', was completed, facing the chapel, with a dormitory on its upper floor, known as Long Chamber, and below part of this a single classroom, Lower School. All the seventy scholars were educated and accommodated in this block.

As the fame of Eton College spread, collegers were joined by commensals, fee-paying boys from further afield, who lodged either in the cloister with the fellows, or in Eton town with a landlady. Commensals were abolished during the Commonwealth, but following the Restoration fee-paying students were again admitted, this time known as oppidans (lodging in the town). After 1772, oppidans boarded in dames houses, expressly run for the college by ladies, or in domines which were run by men in a similar way.

A new classroom block, added in 1670 to the west side, completed the enclosure of School Yard by buildings but this proved to be structurally unsound and was replaced by Upper School in 1694.

Eton continued to flourish until the late 18C and first half of the

19C when conditions, particularly in Long Chamber, had become so bad that by 1841 only half the college vacancies were taken up. In 1846 New Buildings were opened, providing individual rooms for the collegers, and the infamous Long Chamber was partitioned. From then onward Eton expanded at a great rate and additonal buildings were constructed throughout the 19C and 20C.

Eton has provided twenty prime ministers, including Robert Walpole, Pitt the Elder, Lord Gray, Lord Derby, Canning, Gladstone and Macmillan. Writers, Shelley, Fielding, Orwell and Huxley studied at Eton as did the economist Keynes and scientists Boyle and Herschel. The Duke of Wellington is probably the best known of many Old Etonian military leaders.

There are still seventy collegers whose education is paid for by the Foundation but oppidans total almost 1200. Although educating a boy at Eton is expensive, fees are not the highest of all public schools and evidently represent approximately half the cost of sending a boy to Borstal for corrective training!

Boys now wear tail coats and pin-stripe trousers, but the broad 'Eton Collar' was abandoned in the 1960s. Senior boys wear 'stick up' wing collars and white bow ties. Although top hats ceased to be worn early in the Second World War, when it proved impossible for a boy to carry a gas mask as well as a 'topper', they may occasionally be seen on special occasions.

Twenty-four oppidan houses each accommodate around fifty boys who are provided with individual bed-sitting rooms. Collegers have similar rooms, either in Long Chamber, now divided into twenty-one units, or in New Buildings. Boys are taught in numerous classrooms spread throughout the complex. They attend Eton from 13 years old and may stay until they are 18. Each is assigned a tutor who exercises general supervision over his studies.

Windsor

Windsor Castle is England's premier fortress and longest continuously occupied royal residence. Within the castle's precinct lies St George's Chapel, which is the Chapel of the Order of the Garter and a royal mausoleum. The State Apartments are some of the most sumptuously decorated rooms in the country.

Windsor town lies south and west of the castle. Although small, its ancient core retains many buildings of interest.

Windsor Great Park, east of the castle, is the largest of all the royal parks.

Timing Ideally, Windsor Castle should be visited when the State Apartments and St George's Chapel are open (consult the complicated opening details on page 12). To see everything, allow a whole day. The Royal Family gathers at Windsor Castle for Christmas, and the Court moves here at Easter. The Sovereign is also in residence during the Royal Ascot races. Most of the Upper Ward, including the State Apartments, is closed during these periods.

Opening details of the royal buildings

Castle Precinct
Windsor Castle is closed throughout the day of the Garter installation ceremony in June (variable date). As the castle is a private residence, its precinct, or various buildings within it, may, on occasion, be closed at short notice and this should be borne in mind when consulting the following schedule of opening times. Binoculars will prove of great assistance, particularly within St George's Chapel and the State Apartments where much of interest is at a high level. Open daily 10.00. Closes October–March 16.15. April and September 17.15. May–August 19.15. Admission free.

St George's Chapel
Open Monday–Saturday 10.45–15.45, Sunday 14.00–15.45. During British Summer Time the chapel remains open fifteen minutes later. The chapel is closed 2–24 January, and during June for three days preceding, and one day following, the Garter installation ceremony (variable dates). Admission charge. The chapel is also open for services, when there is no admission charge.

Edward IV's Chantry Chapel
This chapel may be visited as part of a guided tour, by appointment or if attending the 08.00 weekday service (11.30 on Friday).

Albert Memorial Chapel
Open Monday–Saturday 10.00–13.00, and 14.00–15.45. Admission free.

Curfew Tower
Open for guided tours only (duration 20 minutes). Tuesday to Saturday at half-hourly intervals from 11.00–12.45 and 14.00–15.45 The tower is not open for most of September. Admission charge.

East Terrace Gardens
The gardens are open to the public on Sundays in August if the weather is fine; a military band frequently entertains.

Queen Mary's Doll's House and the Exhibition of Drawings
Open Monday–Saturday, 10.30–15.00. During British Summer Time the exhibitions are open until 17.00. On the first Sunday in May 13.30–15.00; from the second Sunday in May to the penultimate Sunday in October, Sunday 13.30–17.00. Admission charge to each.

State Apartments
Open 3 January to the second week in March (variable date), Monday–Saturday 10.30–15.00. From the second week in May (variable date) to the first Sunday in June and from the last Saturday in June to the last Saturday in October, Monday–Saturday 10.30–17.00, Sunday 13.00–17.00. From the last Sunday in October to 7 December, Monday–Saturday 10.30–15.00. Admission charge.

Outside Windsor Castle
Royal Mews Museum (St Albans Street)
Details as for Queen Mary's Dolls' House and the Exhibition of Drawings.

Royal Mausoleum (Frogmore)
Open early in May for two days as part of the Frogmore Gardens opening 11.00–19.00. Admission charge. Also on the Wednesday nearest to Queen Victoria's birthday, (24 May), 11.00–16.00. Admission free.

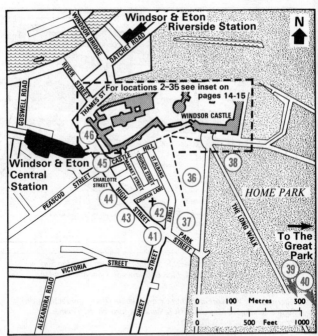

Locations

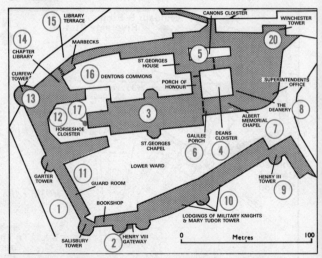

Start *Windsor and Eton Riverside Station (BR) from Waterloo Station
(BR). Exit ahead Datchet Rd. First L Thames St. Continue ahead to
Peascod St (fifth R).*

*Alternatively, Windsor and Eton Central Station (BR) from Paddington
Station (change at Slough). Exit L Station Approach. R. Thames St.
Proceed to Peascod St (first R).*

*Alternatively, Green Line bus 704, 705 or 700 (express, summer only) from
central London to Windsor High Street.*

Locations of interest passed on the route to the castle from Windsor and
Eton Riverside Station are described when they are seen again later.

Location 1	**CASTLE WALLS**

The massive walls, punctuated by bastion towers,
which entirely surround the castle were begun by
Henry II as a defence against his rebellious sons.
The rebellion was soon put down, building work
ceased and the southern section was not built
until the reign of Henry III. The stone used for
the entire wall has always been taken from
Bagshot Heath nearby, and as this is extremely
hard and practically impervious to water it is not
easy to differentiate the periods in which the wall
was built or restored. Most detailing, however,
was executed by *Wyatville* in the 1820s.

A general view of the castle is obtained
immediately from Windsor and Eton Riverside
Station, but when the upper part of Thames
Street is reached, the west section of the wall
predominates. This is seen first if arriving at
Windsor and Eton Central Station or by bus at
Castle Hill.

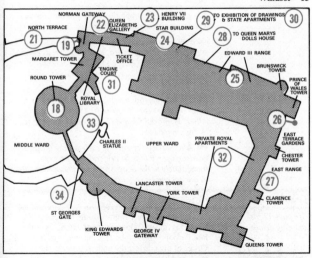

● *View the castle walls from Peascod St as follows:*

The D-shaped tower in the north-west corner is the **Curfew Tower**, followed by the **Garter Tower** and the **Salisbury Tower**. Earlier bastion towers at Windsor had been rectangular, but it was found that rounded towers were harder to damage and also gave the defenders a more extensive view for firing.

Houses clustering around the Curfew Tower were removed in 1863 and the stonework of the tower was then completely renovated.

● *Cross Thames St and follow Castle Hill ahead to the castle's entrance L.*

Location 2	**HENRY VIII GATEWAY**

This forms the main entrance to the castle. Built in 1511, it replaced Henry III's 13C gateway that had fallen into disrepair.

Above the arch are the Tudor Rose of Henry VIII and the pomegranate emblem of Catherine of Aragon, Henry's first consort.

Above the six indentations in the parapet are holes through which boiling liquid could be poured on to attackers.

The room over the gateway was once used as a courtroom.

A portcullis gate originally fitted into the groove which remains within the arch.

•● *Proceed through the gateway. Immediately entered is the Lower Ward, dominated on its north side, ahead, by St George's Chapel. Proceed eastward towards the centre of the chapel to view its exterior.*

•● *Alternatively, if arriving early (the chapel is never open to visitors before 10.45) proceed to the Albert Memorial Chapel (Location 7) and return to this chapel later.*

•● *Alternatively, if arriving early during the peak tourist season it may be preferable to proceed immediately to the State Apartments (Location 30) as queues can be very long.*

Location 3	**ST GEORGE'S CHAPEL**

See page 12 for opening details.

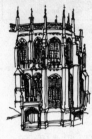

With its outstanding roof vaulting, St George's Chapel is one of England's finest examples of the late Perpendicular style. It is the chapel of the Order of the Garter, the highest order in the land, and here, every June, the Order's annual service is held, when new knights, if any, are installed. Like Westminster Abbey, the chapel also serves as a royal mausoleum and, with the exception of Queen Victoria and Edward VIII (later the Duke of Windsor), all British sovereigns since George II have been buried here. Earlier monarchs also lie in the chapels including two who share the same modest resting place, Henry VIII and Charles I, possibly, for macabre reasons, England's best known kings. St George's Chapel is dedicated to the Virgin Mary, St George and St Edward-the-Confessor. It is a 'Royal Peculiar' i.e. directly responsible to the sovereign.

Edward IV commissioned the chapel as a spiritual centre for the Order of the Garter. He was probably motivated, in part, by the proximity of the splendid College Chapel at Eton, founded by Henry VI, whom he had usurped and allegedly murdered. Building of St George's Chapel commenced in 1475 but was not completed until Henry VIII vaulted the crossing in 1528. During this period, several master masons were employed, including *Henry Jenyngs* and *William Vertue*.

Much restoration has taken place since unsuccessful attempts were made by *Wren* to rectify structural problems in the 17C. This should be borne in mind when examining 'medieval' detailing, both externally and internally.

The design of St George's Chapel is unusually symmetrical for the period, apart from an additional bay allocated to the south-east chapel, and possibly reflects a Renaissance influence.

North and south octagonal chapels protrude from the west end.

North and south transepts divide the nave and chancel (or quire).

A central tower above the crossing was intended but never built.

A south chapel and north vestry protrude at the east end.

•● *Proceed eastward.*

Immediately R of the south chapel is the 13C Galilee Porch (Location 6) which links St George's Chapel with the Albert Memorial Chapel (Location 7) to its east. The south facade of the Albert Memorial Chapel is built entirely in the Perpendicular style.

The Queen's (or King's) Beasts, which surmount the square pinnacles of St George's Chapel's flying buttresses, were made in 1930 as part of restoration work by *Brakspear*.

Similar heraldic animals, first erected in 1557, had been removed by Wren after 1682 to help solve the Chapel's structural problems.

The present beasts bear shields that display the arms of the Houses of Lancaster, York and Tudor.

Carved at low level, in the third bay from the west of the south wall, is the badge of the chapel's founder, Edward IV: a crucifix, rose and rays of the sun. There are six other examples of this badge on the exterior of the building.

Buttresses, parapets and gargoyles are entirely the work of *Pearson*, 1886.

•● *Proceed to the ticket office, L of the south porch, unless attending services which are free.*

The porch was built in 1926.

•● *Enter the chapel.*

The impression of light and space which is immediately gained is typical of late Perpendicular interiors. Master mason *William Vertue* is believed to have been responsible for most of the nave.

Nave. The 'marvel of the chapel' is its palm frond, or waggon head vaulted roof.

Roof bosses in the nave are decorated with: the cross of St George within the Garter, the arms of Henry VIII supported by a dragon and greyhound and the punning rebus of Sir Reginald Bray, a hemp bray (implement for crushing hemp). Bray's rebus is also repeated in stone, glass and iron throughout the nave and within his chapel.

•● *Turn L and proceed westward along the south aisle.*

Nave, south aisle. This, like the north aisle, is fan vaulted.

Towards the end R is the monument to the Prince Imperial of France, d.1879, by *Boehm*. He was the only son of Napoleon III and died fighting for Britain against the Zulus.

The alabaster font at the far end of the aisle is by *Pearson*, 1887.

☛ *Proceed south of the font to the Beaufort Chapel in the south-west corner.*

Beaufort Chapel. Within is the tomb of two ancestors of the dukes of Beaufort: Charles Somerset, Earl of Worcester, d.1526, and his wife, Lady Elizabeth Herbert. Their alabaster effigies are by *Jan van den Einde*.

The bronze grille, *c*.1520, is original, but suffered damage during the Commonwealth and was restored in 1698.

In the niche L stands a 15C Spanish Virgin and Child.

☛ *Proceed to the centre of the nave.*

West window. The west window, with its tracery, was reconstructed by *Willement* in 1845. Glazing had originally begun in 1503 but was not completed until 1509. Fifty-one of the seventy-five stained glass figures are original although some rearrangement has taken place. Popes, kings, princes and saints are depicted.

In the lower corner R, the figure with a hammer is believed to be William Vertue.

☛ *Continue towards the Urswick Chapel in the north-west corner of the north aisle.*

Just before the Urswick Chapel is the statue of Princess Charlotte's consort, Leopold of Saxe-Coburg, who became the first king of the Belgians, by *Boehm*, 1878.

☛ *Continue to the Urswick Chapel.*

Urswick Chapel. Dean Christopher Urswick, who had contributed generously towards the completion of the nave, appropriated this chapel in 1507, although it had been founded by two canons and a verger in 1493 for their own chantry.

Inscribed on the stone base of the screen, made in 1520, is a prayer for Urswick's soul. Until the Reformation this was recited twice daily by the choirboys.

The allegorical marble monument to Princess Charlotte of Wales by *Matthew Wyatt* commemorates the only daughter of George IV, who died in 1817 after giving birth to a stillborn son.

Panel paintings of bishops, *c*.1500, flank the monument. On the wall L is a memorial tablet to George V of Hanover.

The 16C brass lectern R was probably made in the Netherlands.

☛ *Proceed eastward along the north aisle.*

Nave, north aisle. Immediately R is the tomb of George V, d.1936, and Queen Mary, d.1953, by *Lutyens*. Both figures were carved by *Reid Dick* in 1939, and that of Queen Mary added on her death in 1953.

☛ *Continue to the Rutland Chapel in the north transept.*

From the west end of the church, as far as the crossing, a different stone is used from the earlier eastern section of the chapel, indicative of the slowness with which work proceeded.

Rutland Chapel. The transept is not open but its interior may be viewed from the entrance.

Palm frond vaulting continues in this transept.

The stone screen is 16C. It incorporates the Bray rebus in its frieze.

A copper plate on the wall R commemorates the founder of the chapel, Sir Thomas St Leger, who was executed by Richard III in 1483.

In the centre of the chapel are alabaster effigies of George Manners, Lord Roos, d.1513, and Anne, his wife. They were ancestors of the dukes of Rutland, whose chantry chapel this became.

A frieze of demi-angels between the two ranges of east windows, denotes that an altar once stood below.

Immediately R is the choir screen, described later.

➨ *Continue ahead to the George VI Memorial Chapel.*

George VI Chapel. The King died in 1952 but the chapel was not completed until 1969 and his body rested until then in the Royal Vault. Words inscribed R of the gate were spoken by the King in his Christmas broadcast of 1939, the first year of the Second World War.

➨ *Continue eastward along the north aisle of the chancel.*

Chancel, north aisle. Fan-vaulting, continued in the chancel's aisle, was completed in 1480.

Carved on the lower frieze of the north wall are leaves, men and a variety of creatures; all original, unrestored work.

➨ *Proceed to the Hastings Chapel*

Hastings Chapel. This is dedicated to St Stephen. It contains the tomb of William, Lord Hastings, who was summarily executed at the Tower of London by Richard III in 1483. His was the earliest known execution to take place on Tower Green.

Wall paintings depicting St Stephen's martyrdom are by a provincial English artist *c.*1490.

Angel friezes decorate the east and west walls.

➨ *Continue eastward.*

See page 12 for opening details.

Edward IV's Chantry Chapel. The chapel is situated above the last two most easterly bays of the chancel's north aisle and the aisle's ceiling is, therefore, lower at this point.

A small oriel window is fitted at upper level in its west wall. The entrance to the chapel is in the north wall of the north aisle.

Its door is fitted with a 'judas' spy window.

•➤ *Ascend the 18C newel staircase by* Emlyn.

The large oriel window on the east side was originally of stone, like the others, but Henry VIII enlarged and rebuilt it of wood *c.*1520 to form an enclosed pew for his first wife, Catherine of Aragon. Its chief purpose may have been to provide her with a good view of the annual Garter ceremony.

The chapel was converted for George III in 1785 to provide the royal pew.

From here, Queen Victoria witnessed the wedding of her eldest son, the Prince of Wales, later Edward VII, in 1863.

The screen and stalls are by *Emlyn*, 1792.

Return to the chancel's north aisle and proceed eastward passing R the entrance to the choir.

Immediately R is the tomb of Edward IV and his consort, Elizabeth Woodville. The King died in 1483 but this monument was made by *Emlyn* in 1789.

•➤ *Return westward and enter the chancel L.*

Chancel. The chancel was roofed with timber when completed in 1483. Its stone palm frond vault by *William Vertue* replaced this in 1509.

Immediately L, against the north wall, are a pair of 15C gates made by *Joshua Tresilian*, principal ironsmith to Henry VII. They have been judged the finest examples of their type in England. The gates, which originally enclosed Edward IV's tomb in the north aisle, were transferred here in the 18C.

Above are the two south oriel windows of Edward IV's chapel. On Henry VIII's window R Gothic arches are combined with Classical balustrades, denoting a Renaissance influence.

Carvings below include the badges of Henry and Catherine of Aragon.

Two large wooden candlesticks within the sanctuary are copies of those made, in Renaissance style, for Henry VIII *c.*1535; there were originally four.

The reredos by *John Birnie Philip*, 1863, was built as a memorial to the Prince Consort.

New tracery was designed for the east window by *George Gilbert Scott* in 1863 to accommodate stained glass, also commemorating Prince Albert. This replaced a window depicting the Resurrection by *West*.

•➤ *Proceed westward through the choir.*

Choir. An inscribed floor slab covers the lift mechanism of the large burial vault of George III and his family. The vault stretches eastward below the Albert Memorial Chapel. George III, George IV and William IV are amongst those buried within.

Knights Companion of the most noble Order of the Garter assemble in the choir every June (a

variable date) for the annual service of the
Order.

Edward III founded the Order *c*.1348, following
the battle of Crecy in 1346. He is believed to have
been inspired by the legend of King Arthur and
the Knights of the Round Table. A round table,
200 ft in diameter is known to have been made
for the King by 1344. The origin of the Garter
and its motto is uncertain, but the following
account given by Polydore Vergil *c*.1500,
although the most romantic and favoured by
many, is unlikely to be true.

Edward III was dancing with a lady, allegedly
Joan, Countess of Kent, later Princess of Wales.
Noticing that her blue garter had fallen, the
gallant King picked it up and handed it to her. In
doing so he accidentally lifted the lady's skirts to
reveal her legs. The amused onlookers were
rebuked by Edward, 'Honi soit qui mal y pense',
('Shame on him who thinks evil of it') which
became the motto of the Order. The King then
informed the gentlemen present that they would
henceforth be proud to wear the garter as the
badge of a new Order.

However, the earliest illustrations depict a garter
which would not have been worn by ladies and
was more likely to have been part of a knight's
accoutrement, possibly representing unity.

This order of chivalry is the personal gift of the
sovereign and one of only two Great Orders (the
other is the Thistle). Knights of the Order wear
the sash over their left arm, unlike members of
the Lesser Orders who wear the sash over the
right arm. The Garter, of blue velvet, bears the
motto in gold and is held in place below the left
knee by a gold buckle. St George is depicted on
the collar and sash badges. The Order consists of
the sovereign and twenty-five knights, one of
whom will be the Prince of Wales (when there is
one). Foreign rulers and younger royal princes
may also be admitted as supernumeraries. Royal
ladies are the only females who may become
Ladies of the Garter and they also are
supernumeraries. Only twenty-five knights may
exist at one time, although additional non-
Christian 'extra' knights are frequently
appointed.

Founded in the same year as the Order, the
College of St George, which includes the dean
and canons of Windsor, is responsible for the
chapel.

The choir resembles the Henry VII Chapel at
Westminster Abbey in many ways, the Chapel of
the Order of the Bath. Its stalls are not only
exquisitely carved but also adorned with what has
been described as the finest display of heraldic
material in the world.

Central and rear stalls are fitted with misericords
(mercy seats).

The first two stalls at the east end on both sides

were added by *Emlyn c.*1790 and the lowest tiers of desks on both sides were made in the 19C. All the remainder were made between 1478 and 1785, the principal carver being *William Berkeley*.

Each knight occupies one of the top tier stalls on either side, and his helmet, crest and banner surmount its canopy.

The earliest stall plates were enamelled, but during the 17C they began to be painted instead. Enamelling was not resumed until 1905 but has continued ever since. Originally a knight's stall plate was fitted after death, but since 1489 it has been fitted following the knight's installation.

Churchill's stall plate is on the north side, in the fifth bay from the east, two tiers up.

The oldest example, made in 1380, depicts Lord Basset's boars head and is on the south side, seven bays from the west, at the top of the central range. It was transferred here, with others, from the old chapel in 1483.

Both central tiers of stalls are occupied by the Military Knights, minor canons and choirmen.

Choirboys occupy the west end of the two lower tiers.

In the centre of the floor, an inscribed marble slab covers the tomb of Charles I, d.1649, Henry VIII, d.1547, and Henry's third wife, Jane Seymour, who died in 1537 after giving birth to the future Edward VI. Henry VIII had specified a sumptuous tomb for himself but his wishes were not respected by his puritanical son. Originally, the third space was reserved for Henry's sixth wife, Catherine Parr, who outlived him, but she remarried and lies elsewhere. Cromwell allotted her vacant place, just over one hundred years later, to Charles I. This tomb was 'lost' from the 17C until the 19C when it was rediscovered by accident.

Stalls at the west end are those of the royal members of the Order. When royalty is absent their stalls are occupied by the dean and canons who, at other times, are in the sanctuary.

The sovereign's stall is on the south side, immediately L, and the Prince of Wales's on the north side.

●● *Proceed ahead beneath the choir screen.*

The screen, of Coade artificial stone, was made by *Emlyn* in 1792. This is still surmounted by the organ but its pipes were re-aligned in 1930 to provide a complete view of the vaulted roof from both ends of the chapel.

In the last bay of the screen L is a reproduction of the misericord from the sovereign's stall.

Crossing. Henry VIII fan-vaulted the crossing in 1528, thus completing the chapel. The centres of the design are circular whereas the centres of the fan vaults in the aisles are octagonal. The King's arms are carved on the central roof boss, surrounded by those of his Garter Knights.

➤ Enter the Bray Chapel in the south transept.

Bray Chapel. The chapel has been converted to a bookshop. (Bray was very commercially minded and might not have been too upset.) The palm frond vault was completed in 1503.

Sir Reginald Bray, d.1503, is buried here R of the entrance. He was a servant of Henry VII and donated much of the money for building the nave of St George's Chapel. His rebus is carved on the frieze of the screen.

Two canopied niches on the east wall L originally formed part of a stone reredos.

The frieze of demi-angels indicates that an altar once stood here.

Within the chapel are four outstanding wall monuments.

Giles Tomson, d.1612, was Dean of Windsor and Bishop of Gloucester. He is remembered as one of the translators of the King James's Bible and is depicted holding it.

Sir Richard Wortley, d.1603, has a monument which stands in front of a ceramic frame. There were originally four of these in the chapel, believed to be the work of Italian Reanaissance sculptor *Giovanni da Maiano* who was responsible for the roundels at Hampton Court.

The next monument is to Sir William Fitz-Williams, d.1554. Against the west wall of the chapel the monument to Richard Brideoak, d.1678, commemorates a Bishop of Chichester.

➤ Exit from the Bray Chapel R and follow the chancel's south aisle.

Chancel, south aisle. Immediately L is displayed the Panel of the Kings, paintings on wood presented to the chapel in 1492 by Oliver King, a canon of Windsor and Bishop of Bath and Wells; he was also Henry VII's principal secretary. Depicted from L to R, in reverse chronological order, are Henry VII, Edward V (the crown above his head denotes that he was uncrowned), Edward IV and Prince Edward, son of Henry VI. Richard III was omitted for political reasons.

Immediately opposite is the **Oliver King Chapel**, built in 1496. His tomb may lie within.

The stained glass in the window is 15C.

➤ Continue eastward along the aisle to the next bay L.

The painting of Edward III L is believed to be 17C work.

Edward III's battle sword, 6ft 8in (two metres) long, is displayed.

Immediately L is the Oxenbridge Chapel.

Oxenbridge Chapel. John Oxenbridge was canon at Windsor from 1509 to 1522. His rebus, an ox, the letter N and a bridge, are carved over the door.

Demi-angel friezes decorate the east and west walls.

This chapel is dedicated to John the Baptist whose execution is depicted on three panels painted in the Flemish style. One is dated 1422.

● *Continue along the chancel south aisle.*

A rare 17C wooden font occupies the next bay L.

In the following bay L is the stall plate of Thomas Howard, installed as a Knight of the Garter in 1559. He was executed by Elizabeth I in 1572 for planning to marry Mary Queen of Scots. The plate was removed from his stall and fixed here later.

In the south-west corner of the sanctuary is a black slab marking the tomb of Henry VI. The King, allegedly murdered in the Tower of London by Edward IV, was venerated in the early Tudor period but never canonised. His body was brought here in 1484 from Chertsey Abbey by Richard III. Henry VII intended that it should eventually be transferred to Westminster Abbey's Lady Chapel which he rebuilt expressly for this purpose. Following Henry VII's death, however, his son, Henry VIII, decided that Henry VI's body should remain at Windsor.

Many miraculous cures were claimed by those who prayed at this tomb.

On the arch above L is Henry VI's helmet.

Immediately L of the tomb is a 15C wrought iron alms box inscribed with the letter H (for Henry VI).

In the next bay L is the tomb of Edward VII, d.1910, and Queen Alexandra by *MacKennal*, 1919.

Above may be seen a small quatrefoil window in a room over the Lincoln Chapel, seen later.

● *Continue eastward to the last bay of the chancel's south aisle.*

The central stone in the ceiling vault above is unrestored 15C work, carved with the figures of Edward IV and Richard Beauchamp, Dean of Windsor during the construction of the chapel and later Bishop of Salisbury. They are kneeling before a cross, the original of which was presented to the College of St George by Edward III in the 14C and almost certainly stood in St George's Chapel. Made of gold and studded with jewels, it incorporated a wooden fragment, allegedly from the true cross, which had been captured from the last Welsh Prince of Wales and presented to Edward I in 1283. The cross was probably broken up at the Reformation.

● *Proceed to the Lincoln Chapel, in the north-east corner R.*

Lincoln Chapel. This was the first section of St George's Chapel to be completed. It contains the alabaster tomb chest of Edward Clinton, Earl of Lincoln, d.1585, and his third wife, Lady Elizabeth Fitzgerald.

The iron grille is 15C.

In 1481 Edward IV transferred the body of the Rev. John Schorn from North Marston, where he had died in 1314, to a new tomb in this chapel. In his lifetime Schorn had been a famous healer, and the King hoped that his reburial at Windsor would attract more pilgrims and, therefore, more money, which he badly needed so that the building of the chapel might continue. The shrine was probably demolished at the Reformation.

In a casket R is a prayerbook of 1440, acquired in 1949. There is a room above the chapel which may have been connected with pilgrimages to either Schorn or Henry VI. Its west, quatrefoil window has already been seen from the chancel's south aisle.

●● Proceed behind the sanctuary following the ambulatory.

Ambulatory. Much of the east end of the chancel was restored by *George Gilbert Scott* in 1863. The stone screen R by *Brakspear* (?), *c*.1930, conceals the spiral staircase.

The east wall of St George's Chapel, completed in 1248, is its oldest part and originally formed the west wall of Henry III's chapel. Three lancet arches formed the western entrance.

Ironwork on the door is 13C and incorporates the name of *Gilebertus*, the smith who made it. This was gilded in 1955.

Carved on the wall opposite is another example of the cruxifix badge of Edward IV, already seen externally.

Next to this hangs a Mortlake Tapestry, commissioned by Charles I. He originally owned the painting 'Christ at Emmaus' by Titian on which it is based. The tapestry was presented in 1660 by the wife of John, Viscount Mordaunt, governor of Windsor Castle, and hung above the high altar until the 18C.

A floor slab covers the tomb of Sir Jeffry Wyatville, George IV's architect, who was responsible for much of the 19C work at Windsor.

Remains of a 13C Purbeck marble font are displayed against the north wall ahead.

The monument to Robert C. Packe, d.1815, is by *Hopper*. It depicts the dying officer.

●● Return eastward towards the exit door ahead.

Behind this door L is the vestry, 1353 (not open).

Above the exit door are the arms of George III.

●● Exit to Dean's Cloister and follow the west arcade L.

Location 4	**DEAN'S CLOISTER**

The cloister was first built in 1240, but the inner tracery of its arcade was completed in 1345 to provide a covered way from Henry III's chapel to

the Deanery and the former Canons' Lodgings.
The present glazing was completed in 1984.

Most doorways in the walls are 14C.

•● *Proceed to the first passage L in the north-west
corner.*

The vaulted porch, '**The Porch of Honour**',
illustrates the transition from the flowing tracery
of the Decorated style to the less flamboyant
Perpendicular style and is most important
architecturally. This was built in 1353 and has
surprisingly escaped restoration.

Its star-patterned vaulted ceiling represents an
early development of fan vaulting.

Above the porch is the original aerary (treasury)
of 1355. It is now the muniments room and not
open to the public.

Above this is the original Chapter Library, now
the Chapter House and Chapter Clerk's Office,
also not open.

•● *Return to Dean's Cloister. Turn L and
continue towards the barrier. Follow the first
passage L to Canons' Cloister.*

Location 5   **CANONS' CLOISTER**

This cloister's arcade was completed in 1356. Each
of the twelve canons lodged in separate rooms and
their doorways survive in the surrounding walls.

The central passage was rebuilt by *George Gilbert
Scott* in the 19C. He reconstructed timber arches
in the manner of the original roofs, which all the
arcades originally possessed.

•● *Return to the west arcade of Dean's Cloister.*

From here across the garth (central green), may
be seen the cloister's east wall which is also the
west wall of the Deanery. The Deanery, like the
cloister arcade, was built in 1354 and the 14C
vestry of Henry III's chapel is now incorporated
with it.

Ahead, the south wall of the cloister was built in
1248 as the north wall of Henry III's chapel. This
wall has been retained through frequent
rebuilding and now forms the north wall of the
Albert Memorial Chapel.

Its blind arcading is original, although much
restored.

All this wall was once decorated with a fresco
*c.*1270 and a remnant (restored) depicts a king,
either St Edward-the-Confessor, to whom
Henry's chapel was dedicated, or Henry III.

Immediately ahead, in the south-west corner of
the cloister, is the entrance to the Galilee Porch.
Its doorway is 13C.

Location 6   **GALILEE PORCH**

This is believed to have provided a narthex (small
ante chapel) at the west end of Henry III's chapel.

It has been called the Galilee Porch since the 13C.

This is because the leader of processions into the chapel, via the porch, symbolized Christ preceding his disciples into Galilee after the Resurrection.

The ceiling vault was added by Henry VIII in 1511.

On the west wall R is the lancet arch of the central door, flanked by traces of two other lancets. The east side of this wall has already been seen in St George's Chapel.

Ahead, the south entrance to the porch, although much restored, was built by Henry VIII.

The west wall of the Albert Memorial Chapel L also survives from Henry III's Chapel.

Immediately R of the entrance door is a further wall painting, c.1270, which, again, may depict either St Edward-the-Confessor or Henry III.

| Location 7 | **ALBERT MEMORIAL CHAPEL** |

See page 12 for opening details.

This medieval chapel was completely remodelled internally in 1873 as a memorial to the Prince Consort who is, however, buried in a mausoleum, together with Queen Victoria, at Frogmore in Windsor Castle's Home Park.

Henry III completed the first chapel on the site in 1248 and, as has been seen, two walls survive from this building which was dedicated to St Edward-the-Confessor.

Edward III rebuilt the chapel in 1354 for the Order of the Garter and this remained their chapel until 1483. He made it a collegiate church and added the Virgin Mary and St George to the dedication. The chapel later served as the Lady Chapel of the new St George's Chapel but eventually fell into disrepair.

Henry VII began further rebuilding in 1494, but it is probable that elements from Edward's building were retained. No precise records exist of Henry VII's work, and as the Perpendicular style was continued it is not possible to distinguish, with certainty, between Edward's and Henry's periods.

Henry VII originally intended that his building should be a chantry chapel and tomb house for himself and Henry VI. Later he changed his mind and built the Henry VII Chapel at Westminster Abbey for this purpose. As has been seen, however, Henry VI's body remained at Windsor.

Work was still unfinished at Henry VII's death and in 1514 Thomas Wolsey, apart from the King the most powerful figure in the land, acquired the chapel, paid for its completion, and commissioned a huge tomb from Italy which was set up within the chapel in 1529. Almost immediately, however, Wolsey fell out of favour with Henry VIII who appropriated both the chapel and Wolsey's tomb. The tomb remained unused until 1808 when its black marble sarcophagus was converted to form part of Nelson's tomb in St Paul's Cathedral.

Charles II planned to replace the chapel with a new building in honour of his executed father, Charles I, and *Wren* designed a rotunda in 1678. However, this scheme was never proceeded with as Charles II claimed that his father's body could not be found! The money collected was put by the King to more worldly use.

George III considered adapting the chapel as a chapter house for Knights of the Garter but, again, this was never done.

It is immediately apparent that the interior of the chapel is not genuine Gothic but Gothic Revival work. This is because it was completely redecorated by *Henri Triqueti* in 1873, when Queen Victoria decided that it should commemorate her consort, who had died in 1861.

The walls are decorated with marble, carved to depict Biblical scenes, by *Jules Destreez*.

The vaulted ceiling is by *Salvati* with mosaic work by *Triqueti*.

Two large tombs occupy the centre of the chapel.

Prince Leopold, Duke of Albany, d. 1884, by *Boehm*, was Queen Victoria's youngest son. His standard is displayed in front of his tomb.

Prince Albert Victor, Duke of Clarence, d.1892, was the eldest son of Edward VII and heir to the throne. He has been implicated by some of the many writers seeking to throw light on the infamous 'Jack the Ripper' murders at the end of the 19C. The tomb is regarded as the masterpiece of sculptor *Alfred Gilbert*. Gilbert began the monument in 1892 but went bankrupt and fled abroad in 1901. He eventually returned and completed the work by the addition of five statues of saints in 1926.

Its Art Nouveau grille, in continental style, depicts the Tree of Jesse.

Beyond this is the cenotaph of Prince Albert. The figure is by *Triqueti*. This was never used as Albert's tomb; the prince lay in the Royal Vault whilst the mausoleum at Frogmore was under construction.

The reredos, in Sicilian marble, depicting the Resurrection is by *Triqueti* and *Scott* 1872. Edward III's earlier reredos of Nottingham alabaster evidently required eight horses to transport it!

Behind the altar is a further entrance to the Royal Vault, which was created in 1810. It is customary for leading members of the Royal Family to rest within whilst their memorial tombs are being constructed.

•● *Return to the Galilee Porch and exit to the Lower Ward L. Proceed to the Deanery which adjoins the east end of the Albert Memorial Chapel.*

Location 8	**DEANERY**

This was built in 1354 as the chapter house for the Knights of the Garter. At the rear, it incorporates the 14C vestry of the Albert Memorial Chapel. The building is still the dean's residence. Sir Christopher Wren, the architect, spent most of his boyhood in this house as his father was Dean of Windsor from 1635 to 1659.

An original 14C side window of four lights survives.

The large east wing was added *c.*1500.

In front of the house, the sunken courtyard is part of the ditch which, together with a wall, once divided the Lower and Middle Wards.

A 14C gatehouse with a drawbridge stood where the dividing wall runs across the courtyard.

Adjoining the Deanery is the Superintendent's Office, built by *Wyatville* in the 19C on the site of the 17C Guardroom.

●● *Cross to the south-east side of the Lower Ward.*

Location 9	**HENRY III TOWER**

This was completed in 1226. Its great size is evidence of the King's desire to strengthen the castle's defences following two sieges it had withstood during the reign of his father, King John. The two round-headed first floor windows were built by *May* for Charles II in the 17C. Almost all the others at Windsor have since been converted to the Gothic style.

●● *Turn R and return south-westward. Adjoining Henry III's Tower are the Lodgings of the Military Knights.*

Location 10	**LODGINGS OF THE MILITARY KNIGHTS AND MARY TUDOR TOWER**

The Military Knights, who in old age had fallen on hard times, were originally known as Poor or Veteran (*militas pauperi* or *veterani*) and had been established by Edward III with his Garter foundation. One of their duties was to pray daily, at Mass, for the souls of the Garter Knights.

Edward only provided sufficient funds for three knights but Henry VIII, in his will, increased their number to thirteen and decreed that they should be lodged between the Henry III Tower and the Henry VIII Gateway. William IV renamed them Military Knights in 1833 and their successors, retired army officers, still occupy the lodgings. They represent absent Knights of the Garter in St George's Chapel and wear the red uniform of William IV's period.

The first range was built of ragstone in 1359 to accommodate clerks of Henry III's chapel. Conversion for the Poor Knights was completed in 1558. It was heavily restored in 1850.

Blocked arches can be seen on the ground floor.

Following this is the short Mary Tudor Tower, built by Edward III in 1359 as the belfry of Henry III's Chapel. The arms of Mary I and her husband, Philip II of Spain, are carved above the large first floor window. Few examples of Philip's arms survive in this country as the Spanish king launched his armada against England in 1588, thirty years after Mary's death.

Garter House. This adjoins the Mary Tudor Tower, and served as the 19C mess hall of the Military Knights. It is now the residence of the Superintendent of Windsor Castle.

Above the door hangs the badge of the Order of the Garter.

The next range is of ashlar (dressed stone) and was newly built in 1558 to complete the Poor Knights' Lodgings. Its stone was brought from Reading Abbey, which had been demolished at the Reformation.

●● *Continue south-westward, passing the Henry VIII Gateway (Location 2).*

The castle's main bookshop adjoins the gateway.

In the south corner of the Lower Ward is the 13C Salisbury Tower, once occupied by an important Garter official, the Bishop of Salisbury; Windsor then lay in his diocese.

Location 11	**THE GUARD ROOM**

This occupies the south-west side of the Lower Ward between the Salisbury and Garter towers. It was built by *Salvin* in 1862 against a section of the outer wall which, with its towers, had been completed in 1230. When not on duty, members of the castle's guard are based here. Changing of the guard in winter takes place in the foreground.

Garter Tower, also 13C, was formerly the residence of the Garter King of Arms.

Ahead, the timber and brick buildings form the south range of Horseshoe Cloister.

●● *Pass throught the archway to Horseshoe Cloister and proceed clockwise.*

Location 12	**HORSESHOE CLOISTER**

This cloister is unusual in that it is only three-sided and has a unique horseshoe shape, hence its name. It was built by Edward IV in 1481 to provide twenty-one individual houses for the priest vicars of St George's Chapel, predecessors of the minor canons. The verger, lay clerks, sacristans and choirmen now occupy these houses.

All were heavily restored in the 19C.

●● *Follow the next covered passage L, on the north-east side of the cloister. Behind this lies the Curfew Tower.*

Location 13	**CURFEW TOWER** *1220*

See page 12 for opening details.

This probably replaced an earlier Norman tower. It has served as the bell tower of St George's Chapel since 1477. The Curfew Tower was remodelled in 1863 by *Salvin* who added the gabled roof, inspired by the design of a bastion tower in the wall of Carcassone, south-west France.

•➡ Await the guide in Horseshoe Cloister where a clock indicates the time of the next tour. Enter at ground floor level.

The wooden internal structure was erected in the 15C in connection with the conversion of the building to a bell tower. Previous to this, it had served as a storehouse.

A lectern and steps, *c.*1760, in Neo-Gothic style, are displayed.

The stairs were made *c.*1300.

The clock and chime mechanisms of 1689 survive, although they are now powered by electricity. Eight times daily, at three hourly intervals from midnight, the hymn 'St David's' is played, followed by the peal 'The King's Change'.

A cannon of 1550 points eastward over the castle; it has never been fired.

Romanesque arches are a surprising feature of the tower, as by 1220 the pointed Gothic arch was practically ubiquitous.

At this level, the walls are 13 ft thick.

The vaulted bays are believed to have served as prison cells, particularly during the Civil War period. However, allegations that Anne Boleyn was imprisoned here are untrue.

Displayed are mantraps and stocks.

•➡ Return to Horseshoe Cloister L. Pass through the next arch L in the north corner of the cloister to Denton's Commons. Immediately L is the stone-built Chapter Library (not open).

Location 14	**CHAPTER LIBRARY** *1415*

The building may originally have served as a hall for the priest vicars and clerks. It has been the Chapter Library since 1694.

•➡ Ascend the steps L to the Library Terrace.

Location 15	**LIBRARY TERRACE**

Immediately below the steep escarpment lies Thames Street and the town of Windsor. Across the river, immediately northward, is Eton's College Chapel dominating the college complex. In the distance are the Chiltern hills.

•➡ Return to Denton's Commons to view the north range of houses (no entrance to this area which is private). The first house is Marbeck's.

| Location 16 | **DENTON'S COMMONS** |

Marbeck's, the large, much restored timber and brick house was built in the 15C, probably as a communal dining room for the priest vicars and choristers. Its name commemorates a 16C resident, John Marbeck, Master of the Choristers. He was condemned to be burnt at the stake as a heretic by Henry VIII in 1543, but gained a reprieve due to his musical skills.

The house is still the home of the Organist and Master of the Choristers.

Denton's Commons was once occupied by Henry II's ceremonial apartments which included the Great Hall. The hall was built of stone in 1171 and survived the fire of 1226 when most other buildings in the Lower Ward were destroyed. It lay between the present houses and the north wall of St George's Chapel (built later). The hall was adapted for the chantry priests in 1520 and called Denton's Commons, to commemorate Canon James Denton. Demolition of the building took place in 1859.

Some of the hall's stonework and a 14C window survive in an external wall of the rambling building adjoining Marbeck's.

A 17C house with Classical brick pilasters follows.

Facing west is **St George's House**, also 17C and of brick but stuccoed later. This was built in 1661, as his residence, by Dr George Hall, Bishop of Chester and Canon of Windsor.

Its rear section incorporates a mid-14C building. The hall now serves as a conference centre.

Forming the south side of Denton's Commons is the north wall of St George's Chapel.

•• *Return to Horseshoe Cloister. Immediately L is the west front of St George's Chapel.*

| Location 17 | **ST GEORGE'S CHAPEL WEST FRONT** |

The west front was not completed until 1511.

Above the window are statues of the chapel's patron saints: St George, the Virgin Mary and St Edward-the-Confessor. They are of Coade stone and were added in 1799.

Steps and the west approach were originally designed by *George Gilbert Scott* in 1870 but completely rebuilt in 1981.

This entrance is only opened on ceremonial occasions, and, according to Queen Victoria's diary, it was used for the first time since the chapel was built for the wedding of her daughter, Princess Louise, in 1871.

Two small rooms which flank the staircase were built as individual living quarters for chantry priests. Each retains its fireplace and a niche to accommodate a bed.

•• *Return to Lower Ward L. Pass the south wall of St George's Chapel and continue ahead to Middle Ward. Immediately ahead is the Round Tower.*

Location 18	**ROUND TOWER**

Not open.

This tower is the keep of Windsor Castle and forms the core around which it is built. Edward III lived here in the mid 14C while the royal apartments were being reconstructed. Later it became the governor's residence and, at one stage, accommodated distinguished prisoners. The Round Tower now houses the Royal Archives and is not, therefore, open to the public.

William the Conqueror created the motte (mound), surmounted by a wooden structure, *c.*1070. Henry II replaced this with a stone tower to strengthen the castle's defences. It is believed to have been a 'shell' keep enclosing timber buildings. Most of the stonework was renewed by *May* in the 17C, but the tower was, until the 19C, only half the height of the present structure.

When the east and south ranges of the Upper Ward were converted to private apartments for George IV a storey was added to them and new towers and battlements built. This work would have made the Round Tower appear insignificant and *Wyatville* therefore doubled its height *c.*1827.

As with the castle wall, Bagshot Heath stone has always been used and it is, therefore, difficult to distinguish between the building periods.

The flagpole was erected in 1892 and the Royal Standard flies from this when the sovereign is in residence. At other times, the Union Jack is hoisted.

Internally, much of the two-storey, mid-14C timber structure survives. A well descends from one room to the River Thames below and this is believed to have been the only source of water available to the Norman garrison.

An 18C bell, made in Moscow and known as the Sebastopol Bell, was captured in the Crimean War and brought to the Round Tower. It only tolls on the death of a sovereign.

The moat garden marks the position of the original defensive ditch.

North of the Round Tower is the short **Magazine Tower**, *c.*1357 with 19C additions.

The wall between is part 12C and part 14C.

•• *Proceed clockwise to the Norman Gateway ahead.*

Location 19	**NORMAN GATEWAY**

This forms the entrance to the Inner Ward and was built in 1359. The gateway was probably called 'Norman' as it is close to Henry II's Norman Round Tower.

A wooden portcullis remains in position within the arch and its lower edge is visible.

The north tower's ground floor is original and retains a vaulted ceiling. Above this, the structure is by *Wyatville*.

The south tower and the section above the arch are original, apart from the top floor which has been rebuilt.

This gateway served as a prison until the 17C. King Jean of France and his son Philippe were imprisoned here after being captured at Poitiers by Edward III in 1356. They shared the prison with King David II of Scotland who had been captured ten years earlier.

James I of Scotland was interned here for eleven years from 1413 to 1424. He observed Lady Joan Beaufort walking below in the garden at the foot of the Round Tower, fell in love with her and eventually married her.

The gatehouse now forms part of the governor's residence. Within, are examples of prisoners' graffiti.

●● *Return westward, turn R and proceed to the North Terrace. Turn L and continue ahead to the Winchester Tower at the west end of the terrace.*

Location 20 | **WINCHESTER TOWER**

This tower was originally built in the 12C and, although reconstructed in 1356, its wall displays more of Henry II's work than elsewhere at Windsor. Some original stone blocks and narrow flint bonds survive.

The Clerk of Works in 1356 was William of Wykeham and his work is commemorated on the north side by the Latin words 'Hoc Fecit Wykeham Anno Domini 1356' ('This was made by Wykeham in AD1356'). The inscription was re-cut in the 19C but may not be accesible.

Return eastward along the terrace.

Location 21 | **NORTH TERRACE**

A terrace was originally constructed in timber at this point by Henry VIII in 1533, but it was rebuilt in stone by Elizabeth I in 1578. Charles II widened the terrace and extended it around the quadrangle in the Upper Ward when he built new royal apartments.

Before this terrace was formed the castle's north wall ascended directly from the sheer slopes of the escarpment.

Near this point 'one hundred steps' descend to Windsor town, via a 19C bastion tower. This route was once popular with Eton schoolboys as public entrances to the castle were 'out of bounds'. Here, on the terrace, George III, a great supporter of the college, would chat with the boys, frequently inviting them to dine with him in the castle.

●● *Proceed eastward along the terrace passing the Norman Gateway R. Attached to the gateway's east side is Queen Elizabeth's Gallery.*

Location 22	**QUEEN ELIZABETH'S GALLERY**

This building was constructed by Elizabeth I in 1583. Its first floor was remodelled in 1834, together with that of the adjacent Henry VII building, to accommodate the royal library.

Tickets for the State Apartments, Queen Mary's Dolls' House and the Exhibition of Drawings can only be purchased at the foot of this building, R of the steps.

●● *Immediately ahead R is the Henry VII Building.*

Location 23	**HENRY VII BUILDING**

Henry VII required additional accommodation for his growing family and took advantage of a gap in the castle buildings at this point by constructing this three-storey block. Its first floor now links with Queen Elizabeth's Gallery to provide the royal library.

●● *Continue ahead.*

Location 24	**STAR BUILDING**

This completely new structure was built for Charles II by *May*, *c.*1675 to accommodate many of the royal apartments. All the windows were converted to the Gothic style in the 19C.

The entrance to the State Apartments and Exhibition of Drawings is situated in this building.

●● *Continue past the entrance to Queen Mary's Dolls' House to the Edward III range.*

Location 25	**EDWARD III RANGE**

The range was completely remodelled in the 19C although much of the wall fabric is 14C.

Passed R are the **Cornwall** and **Brunswick Towers**, the latter entirely the 19C work of *Wyatville*.

●● *If the Royal Family are not in residence continue ahead following the East Terrace to the barrier.*

Part of the terrace at this point passes over the roof of an orangery built for George IV when the formal gardens were created.

Location 26	**EAST TERRACE GARDENS**

In the gardens are four 17C bronze statues made for Charles II by *Le Sueur*. They originally stood in the garden of St James's Palace.

The four early-18C lead vases between the statues were designed by the Dutch sculptor *Van Mieris*. The central vase, depicting 'The Judgement of Paris', was made by *Pearce c.*1690.

Immediately surrounding the terrace is the Home Park, private to the Royal Family.

Overlooking the gardens is the east range of the castle which accommodates the private apartments of the Royal Family.

Location 27	**EAST RANGE**

Although originally built by Henry II, as indicated by the rectangular towers, no vestige of Norman detailing remains.

All the oriel windows were added by *Wyatville* when he adapted the range for royal occupancy in the 1820s.

The entire top storey is also a *Wyatville* addition.

The towers in this facade are described as seen L to R.

The **Queen's Tower** was built by *May* in 1680 as a replacement for a Norman tower. It was first known as the New Tower and later, in honour of Queen Victoria, the Victoria Tower.

The **Clarence Tower** retains two tall windows which were probably added by *May*.

The **Chester** and **Prince of Wales Towers** follow.

Beginning in 1804, *Wyatt* had already completed some external work for George III using white Portland stone dressings. *Wyatville*, beginning in 1820, used brown sandstone.

●● *Return to the North Terrace. The first public doorway L is the entrance to Queen Mary's Dolls' House. It is more convenient to see this before the State Apartments.*

●● *Alternatively, if not viewing the Dolls' House, continue westward and proceed to the next doorway L, the entrance to the State Apartments and the Exhibition of Drawings. If viewing both, enter the Drawings Exhibition first.*

●● *Alternatively, if not visiting the castle's interiors, continue ahead and ascend the next stairway L beneath Queen Elizabeth's Gallery to Engine Court R. Visitors to the State Apartments will exit at almost the same point (Location 31).*

Location 28	**QUEEN MARY'S DOLLS' HOUSE**
See page 12 for opening details.	The dolls' house was presented by the nation to Queen Mary, consort of George V, in 1923. It was not her childhood toy as many believe. The architect, *Lutyens*, supervised its design in which everything is made to scale (twelve to one). Pictures on the walls include miniature paintings by *A. J. Munnings*.

Kipling and *Chesterton* are two of the authors who wrote special works for the one-inch high library books in which they are inscribed.

Dolls in national costume, displayed in the next room, are from the collection of Elizabeth II.

●● *Proceed to the Exhibition of Drawings which may be followed immediately by the State Apartments.*

●● *Alternatively, exit L and proceed to Engine Court (Location 31).*

| Location 29 | **EXHIBITION OF DRAWINGS** |

See page 12 for opening details.

The exhibition, selected from the Royal Collection, includes works by *Leonardo da Vinci*, *Holbein* and *Michelangelo*.

•● *Proceed to the State Apartments.*

•● *Alternatively, exit L and proceed to Engine Court (Location 31).*

| Location 30 | **STATE APARTMENTS** |

See page 12 for opening details.

These rooms, many of which originally served as the sovereign's private suite, are amongst the most sumptuously decorated in England. They include examples of the 17C carving of *Grinling Gibbons* and ceilings painted by *Verrio*. Although the pictures and furnishings displayed are frequently changed, outstanding works by *Lawrence*, *Holbein*, *Rembrandt*, *Rubens* and *Van Dyck* are generally to be seen.

This north-east section of the escarpment is the highest point on which Windsor Castle is built and, therefore, the most difficult to attack. For this reason it is believed that the royal domestic quarters have always been situated here.

Henry I had accommodation at Windsor when he held his first court here in 1110. Henry II rebuilt this of Bedfordshire stone *c.*1171 and further reconstruction took place by Henry III in the 13C. Edward III rebuilt and extended the apartments on the north side in the 14C. Much of the medieval fabric survives in the walls but only a fragment of early detailing is visible.

Charles II commissioned *Hugh May* to remodel the apartments and construct a completely new range, the four-storey Star Building, on the north side in 1675. The subsequent layout of the apartments has been little changed. George IV transferred the royal private apartments to the east side of the castle and most of the old rooms were converted by *Wyatville* to provide suites for visiting royalty. Three ceremonial rooms were retained as such but they, too, were completely re-designed. Only three rooms retain their 17C decor.

China Museum. Displayed are some of the porcelain services used for important banquets.

Grand Staircase. Earlier staircases to the apartments had lacked grandeur and Queen Victoria commissioned the present structure from *Salvin* in 1866. An open courtyard, Brick Court, had stood here since medieval times and aromatic herbs were grown in its garden to perfume the air. The court was not roofed over until this staircase was built.

•● *Ascend the stair to the first landing.*

Armour from the royal collection is displayed throughout the first areas visited.

The statue of George IV R is by *Chantrey*.

Beneath this stands a suit of armour made for Henry VIII at Greenwich *c.*1540.

The gold inlaid sword in the case below was also made in the 16C for Henry VIII. It commemorates the siege of Boulogne and is the work of the Spaniard *Diego de Cayas*.

•• *Ascend the steps and proceed L to the Grand Vestibule.*

Grand Vestibule. This chamber, in Neo-Gothic style, was designed by *James Wyatt c.*1800 as the landing for a staircase which he built for George III. Wyatt was the uncle of Wyatville who changed his name from Wyatt.

Displayed are two sedan chairs and the vestments of George IV.

On the table L is the 18C sword, with a 16C blade, which was submitted to Lord Louis Mountbatten by the Japanese when they surrendered in 1945.

Behind this, against the north wall, is a statue of Queen Victoria by *Boehm*, 1871.

In the display case L of the door is the bullet that killed Nelson.

The statue of Charles I by *Bird*, 1695, is reputedly a copy of a work by *Bernini*.

William III's statue is an original work by *Bird*, 1695.

Waterloo Chamber. This is one of the three rooms seen before the private apartments that are still used on various ceremonial occasions.

The Waterloo Chamber occupies the site of the second courtyard around which the royal apartments were built. This had been known as Horn Court, due to the antlers which were hung on the walls, much of which retain their 12C fabric. The courtyard was roofed over to form a gallery that would accommodate the portraits, commissioned by George IV from *Sir Thomas Lawrence*, in honour of those who contributed to the defeat of Napoleon. The paintings remain in this room. Commemorative Waterloo banquets are still held annually at Windsor, either here or in the State Dining Room. Work here was not completed until after the King's death but the chamber was again redesigned by *Blore* in 1861.

Fretwork added to the upper parts of the walls was allegedly based on Prince Albert's suggestions.

The carpet, one of the world's largest seamless examples, measures 80 ft by 40 ft and was made in India for Queen Victoria *c.*1850.

Wyatville brought the woodcarving by *Gibbons* from other rooms which he had remodelled.

Garter Throne Room. New Knights Companion of the Order of the Garter are invested here prior to their installation in St George's Chapel. Existing members attend the ceremony.

This room also serves from time to time as the sovereign's private cinema.

The room had been divided for Charles II where the present arch stands; the section entered served as his Presence Chamber and the further smaller section formed part of his Audience Chamber.

Portraits of sovereigns from George I to Queen Victoria, wearing their Garter robes, are hung.

The State Portrait of Elizabeth II is by *James Gunn*.

Grand Reception Room. The room had been Charles II's Guard Chamber, but after the Waterloo Chamber was completed it was planned that this should be used to receive guests to functions held there

The decor, by *Wyatville* in the Louis XV style, was designed to accommodate the recently purchased 18C Gobelin tapestries, part of a set which depicts the story of 'Jason and the Golden Fleece'.

Like the Waterloo Chamber, this room was completed after the death of George IV.

Its north window is a *Wyatville* addition.

Above the fireplaces are 'oriental' clocks from the Brighton Pavilion.

St George's Hall. This hall has always served as the principal banqueting room at Windsor since it was constructed by Edward III in the 14C, and much of the original fabric survives in the walls. It was doubled in size by George IV when he extended it westward in 1829 by absorbing the sovereign's private chapel.

Wyatville's decor is in the Gothic Revival style.

Displayed on the ceiling, walls and window recesses are shields of every Knight of the Garter (more than 900) since the Order was founded.

Above the gallery, at the east end of the hall, is an organ which also serves a private chapel built for Queen Victoria. This lies on the other side of the wall but is not open.

The ceiling appears to be of timber but is, in fact, plaster.

Paintings of Stuart and Hanoverian monarchs include works by *Kneller* and *Lely*.

The most important of the many Hanoverian busts is that of George II (not George I as inscribed on the 19C pedestal) by *Roubiliac* c.1763, it stands L of the exit.

As redesigned in Baroque style for Charles II by *May*, the sovereign's domestic chapel that had occupied the western half of the hall was evidently the most outstanding of the 17C private apartments. Its ceiling by *Verrio* has been lost, but much of the carving by *Gibbons* was re-used, as has been seen, in the Waterloo Chamber.

Queen's Guard Chamber. This is the first of the smaller domestic apartments to be visited. It was customary at Windsor for the queen to be

assigned rooms on the south side whilst the king occupied those on the north side. Originally, this chamber accommodated the queen's bodyguard drawn from the Yeomen of the Guard. George III converted it to a temporary domestic chapel in the late 18C to replace Charles II's Baroque chapel which had become too dilapidated. George IV restored it to appear once again as a guard room, for historical reasons, and to display naval and military trophies.

The bay window, by *Wyatville*, was added specificially to accommodate a section of one of HMS *Victory*'s masts but this eventually perished and was removed in the late 19C.

Remaining in their original positions are the marble busts of Marlborough and Wellington.

Above them hang their standards which are renewed annually by the present dukes. These standards are the 'quit rent' demanded by the sovereign for royal estates leased to their descendants in perpetuity. The Marlborough standard is delivered to Windsor Castle on 13 August, the anniversary of the battle of Blenheim, as rental for the estate of Blenheim Palace at Woodstock. The Wellington standard is delivered, usually by the present Duke in person, on 18 June, the anniversary of the battle of Waterloo. This is the rent for the estate of Stratfield Saye in Hampshire.

Below the Duke of Marlborough's bust is that of his descendant, Sir Winston Churchill, by *Nemon*. This was commissioned by Elizabeth II in 1953 specifically to stand here.

In the centre of the bay is a model of an equestrian figure representing the King's (or Queen's) Champion.

To conclude the feasts at Westminster Hall, which once traditionally followed the coronation ceremony, a knight would enter on horseback, fling down his gauntlet and challenge to a duel anyone who disputed the new sovereign's right to the throne. William IV discontinued the Westminster Hall banquets due, it is believed, to the drunken behaviour which became practically riotous during George IV's coronation feast in 1821.

The model's suit of armour was made in 1585 for Sir Christopher Hatton, Lord Chancellor and a favourite of Elizabeth I. It was worn by the King's Champion at George I's coronation banquet.

The central chair, R of the model, was made from a Waterloo elm tree.

Queen's Presence Chamber. This is the first of three surviving rooms that retain their 17C decor. Much of the wall fabric of this, and the next two rooms survives from the building erected by Edward III as a nursery wing in the 14C.

All the windows of the private apartments had been designed for Charles II in Classical style by

May to harmonize with his interiors, but these were remodelled in the late 18C for George III who wanted to restore the Gothic appearance of the castle's exterior.

The Queen's Page of the Presence would receive visitors here, convey their names to the queen and establish whether or not she would grant them audience.

The ceiling painting by *Verrio* depicts Catherine of Braganza.

Its cove incorporates the monogram of Charles II.

Much of the carving around the picture frames is the work of *Gibbons*, although some is by *Phillips*, and restoration and alteration took place in the 19C.

Gobelin tapestries, completed in 1785, depict the story of King Ahasnerus and Queen Esther. They continue in the next room.

The fireplace, by *Robert Adam*, was brought here from Buckingham Palace by William IV in the 19C.

R of the exit door is a bust of Handel by *Roubiliac*.

Queen's Audience Chamber. This, the second 17C interior to be seen, was where the queen, seated on a throne, would receive her visitors.

Further tapestries from the series seen in the previous room are hung, and again, the ceiling by *Verrio* (much restored) depicts Catherine of Braganza.

Carvings by *Gibbons* and *Phillips* decorate the room.

Displayed is a cabinet that belonged to Mary Queen of Scots.

Queen's Ball Room. The ceiling cove is decorated with the arms of George III who commissioned the three crystal chandeliers in 1804 to encourage their manufacture in England.

Van Dyck portraits are generally displayed.

On the chimney-piece, a French 18C clock is operated by the native's earring.

Two sets of silver dining tables and mirrors are displayed, made for William III and Charles II. The latter was allegedly presented to the King by the City of London.

Queen's Drawing Room. This is the first room entered in the north range, which was built as a completely new structure for Charles II. The queen would withdraw here, either from her Audience Chamber or the adjoining King's Dining Room.

This eventually became one of the drawing rooms in the suite converted by *Wyatville* for visiting royalty.

Most of the decor is earlier work completed by

Wyatt for George III but the ceiling is by *Wyatville*.

The monograms of William IV, in whose reign this room was completed, and his consort, Queen Adelaide, are featured in the ceiling cove.

Paintings by *Holbein* are generally displayed.

The door immediately L of the entrance originally led to the Queen's Bedroom which now forms part of the Royal Library (not open) in the Henry VII building.

The door R of the entrance leads to the Cabinet between the King's Dining Room and the Queen's Drawing Room.

Carved arms and busts by *Gibbons*, possibly re-set, are displayed.

King's Closet. This was Charles II's sitting room and some of his prized possessions were kept here. It later became a bedroom in the state suite.

The arms and monogram on the ceiling are those of Queen Adelaide.

Paintings by *Canaletto* are generally displayed.

King's Dressing Room. Charles II slept in this room, which originally stretched further back. It was reduced in size by *Wyatville* to provide space for bathrooms and only then was it used as a dressing room.

Arms and monograms on the ceiling are those of William IV.

In this room are hung some of the most important paintings in the royal collection including works by *Rembrandt* and *Rubens*. They are frequently changed.

The famous triple portrait of Charles I by *Van Dyck* was a study for a bust.

King's State Bedchamber. The most intimate matters of state were frequently discussed in state bedchambers. Charles II preferred to sleep in greater privacy and, therefore, never used the State Bed which, however, remained here. Following George IV's remodelling, the room was at last used as a bedchamber.

The French 18C bed, believed to be the work of *Georges Jacob*, was first positioned in this room for the Empress Eugenie when she accompanied her consort, Napoleon III, on his state visit to Queen Victoria in 1855. The hangings were made for this occasion. The bed's last occupant was the King of Portugal in 1909.

On the ceiling, in the corners, are the arms of Charles II.

President de Gaulle presented the Aubusson carpet to Elizabeth II during his state visit in 1960.

King's Drawing Room. Charles II would withdraw here from his Audience Chamber, now part of the Garter Throne Room, which was reached through the door opposite the exit or from his dining room (seen next).

The bay window was added by *Wyatville* when the room was remodelled to form a further drawing room for the visitors' suite.

Carved on the ceiling are the arms and monogram of George IV whose body lay in state here following his death at Windsor in 1830.

The carpet was presented to Edward VII by the Shah of Persia in 1903.

King's Dining Room. This, the last room to be visited, retains most of its 17C decor.

Originally, the room's windows overlooked Brick Court but these were filled after the court was roofed over to accommodate the Grand Staircase. In consequence, artificial lighting is now required.

In the reign of Charles II, as in earlier times, the sovereign would eat here in public, and privileged members of society were invited to witness the event. The room, therefore, was known as the King's Public Dining Room.

The ceiling painting by *Verrio* depicts, appropriately, a banquet of the gods.

Carving around the doorways and above the 18C fireplace by *Gibbons*, and much restored, continues the theme of food and drink.

Late 17C Flemish tapestries incorporate the arms of William III.

Displayed in a case R of the exit are a pair of silver-mounted bellows that allegedly belonged to Nell Gwynn.

Exit Staircase. Tapestries made at Old Windsor in 1878 illustrate from R to L Windsor Castle, Balmoral and Buckingham Palace. The last depicts the east range as it was designed by *Blore* for Queen Victoria. Its remodelling for George V in 1913 provided the very different facade that survives today.

Past the foot of the stairs, through an opening L, is the **Grand Entrance Hall** which is not open to the public.

Its vaulted roof formed part of Edward III's 14C building and although much restored is the only medieval detailing in the State Apartments to survive.

☛ *Exit to Engine Court R*

Location 31	**ENGINE COURT**

This is the only original courtyard in the Upper Ward that has not been roofed over.

☛ *Return westward.*

Passed R are the Henry VII building and Queen Elizabeth's Gallery. ER (Elizabeth Regina) and 1583 are inscribed on the wall of the latter.

Ahead is the Norman Gateway.

On the south side of the court is the entrance to the Round Tower (not open).

From the east side, through the railings, may be viewed the Quadrangle with the State Apartments L and the Private Royal Apartments ahead and R.

| Location 32 | **PRIVATE ROYAL APARTMENTS** |

No buildings stood against the Norman wall at this point until Edward III built there in the 14C.

The projecting range that runs around the inside of the east and south ranges was added by *Wyatville* to provide a gallery which would connect the newly formed royal apartments.

A top storey was added to both the east and south range by *Wyatville* for servants' accommodation. This, as can be seen, does not extend above his corridor extension.

In the south-east corner is the sovereign's private entrance.

The south range R accommodates guests of the Royal Family.

The central **George IV Gate**, by *Wyatville*, serves as the ceremonial entrance. This gateway is flanked by twin towers; on the west side, the **Lancaster Tower** is by *Wyatville* but the east **York Tower** was constructed by Edward III.

The most westerly tower in the south range is known as the **Edward III Tower** although it was actually built during the reign of Henry III.

Overlooking the Quadrangle is the statue of Charles II.

| Location 33 | **CHARLES II STATUE** *Ibach 1688* |

This equestrian statue, erected to commemorate the rebuilding of the royal apartments, was paid for by Tobias Rustat, the King's Yeoman of the Robes.

A model for the work was made in wood, allegedly by a German relative of the sculptor.

Panels on the pedestal were carved by *Gibbons*.

➡ *Continue ahead, following the Moat Path (this is closed when a member of the Royal Family is in residence). Proceed to St George's Gate.*

➡ *Alternatively, if the Moat Path is closed, proceed westward through the Norman Gateway and continue anti-clockwise around the Round Tower to St George's Gate.*

| Location 34 | **ST GEORGE'S GATE** *Wyatville* |
| Not open to the public. | This was constructed to give direct access from the castle to the town. |

Above the arch, carved panels depict St George slaying the dragon.

➡ *Exit from the castle precinct through the archway south-west of St George's Gate to Castle Hill. Turn R and follow the south wall of the castle.*

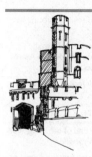

The first section of the wall was rebuilt in the 18C.

The large Henry III Tower and the small drum tower (Garter House) are passed.

Windows in the walls between the Henry III Tower and the Henry VIII Gateway are part of the Military Knights' Lodgings.

•● *Continue ahead through the railings passing R the Henry VIII Gateway.*

Changing of the guard takes place here on the green in summer.

•● *First L St Albans St.*

Location 35	**ROYAL MEWS MUSEUM**
St Albans Street *See page 12 for opening details.*	The mews were built by *Blore* in 1842. Various royal coaches are displayed in the museum including the Scottish State Coach. Some of the gifts presented to Elizabeth II to mark her Silver Jubilee in 1977 are exhibited. •● *Exit L. First L Park St.*
Location 36	**PARK STREET**
	This cul-de-sac, which leads to Windsor Great Park, retains several period houses of note. On the corner R, the stucco block, **Nos 12–16**, is early 19C. Much of the north side is made up of three terraces of modern houses, built in early-18C style. Towards the end, however, are **Nos 23–24**, built in the mid 18C. The **Two Brewers** is an early 17C (?) inn which retains much character. In the 18C it was a coffee house. Opposite, are **Nos 3** and **4**, mid-Georgian but divided by a Neo-Gothic oriel window. •● *Enter the Great Park from Cambridge Gate ahead.*
Location 37	**THE GREAT PARK**
	The park covers 4800 acres of grass and woodland, much of which is open to the public. It is all that remains of a vast hunting forest. Immediately surrounding the castle, the grounds are known as the Home Park. Ahead, running from north to south, is the Long Walk along which the sovereign drives during Royal Ascot week *en route* to the racecourse. An open carriage is used for the last part of the journey. Three miles distant at the end of the Long Walk, on top of Snow Hill, is the statue of George III by *Westmacott*, 1830, commonly referred to as 'The Copper Horse'. The King is depicted without stirrups not, as is often alleged, because he was a good horseman, but because stirrups were unknown in the Roman times the statue's style is derived from. It was from here that Elizabeth II

lit the first of a chain of bonfires to celebrate her Silver Jubilee in 1977.

Motor vehicles are only generally allowed through the park on the main Windsor to Ascot road and at various car parks.

•• Turn L to view the south facade of Windsor Castle.

Location 38	**WINDSOR CASTLE SOUTH FACADE**

The castle's entrance at the end of the Long Walk is the George IV Gate by *Wyatville*.

Guests of the Royal Family occupy the rooms on this side.

Much of the wall fabric is 14C but everything was remodelled by *Wyatville* in the 19C. The top storey is entirely his work.

•• To reach Frogmore House and grounds, in which stands the royal mausoleum, proceed southward following the Long Walk. Turn L before the George III statue. NB: the opening of Frogmore grounds is at present strictly limited.

Location 39	**FROGMORE HOUSE**

The house was designed by *May*, Charles II's architect, in 1680. Extensions and remodelling by *J. Wyatt* for Queen Charlotte in 1792 had disguised its origins until recently.

Outstanding murals by *Laguerre*, illustrating scenes from Virgil's *Aeneid*, were discovered in 1985 and are under restoration. Work is scheduled for completion in 1988 and it is expected that the house will then be opened to groups during August and September.

In the grounds is the royal mausoleum.

Location 40	**ROYAL MAUSOLEUM** *Humbert and Grüner 1871*

See page 12 for opening details.

The mausoleum was commissioned by Queen Victoria to house the tombs of Prince Albert and herself as she did not wish to spend eternity in St George's Chapel with 'those wicked Hanoverian uncles'. Its interior is in Italian Renaissance style.

Effigies on the tomb chests are by *Marochetti*.

Nearby, in the grounds, a simple tombstone marks the burial place of Edward VIII (later the Duke of Windsor).

•• Return to Park St. First L Sheet St.

Facing Victoria St (first R) is **Hadleigh House**, on the east side L, one of Windsor's finest late-18C residences.

•• Return northward. First L High St.

Location 41	**HIGH STREET**

Windsor's relatively short High Street ends at Castle Hill and then becomes Thames Street. Most buildings date from the late 18C and 19C. Houses of interest are on the east side L.

No 4, early 19C, has Neo-Gothic balcony railings.

No 11 is late 18C. Its stucco facade is embellished with reliefs below the upper floor window.

No 13, *c*.1840, has a good balcony.

Opposite, on the west side, is St John-the-Baptist.

Location 42	**ST JOHN-THE-BAPTIST** *Hollis 1822*

High Street

Brass rubbings may be made from Easter to November, Monday–Saturday.

The building, reputedly designed under the supervision of *Wyatville*, replaced an earlier parish church which stood on the site.

●● *Enter the church.*

Within the porch L is the monument to Nazareth Harris, d.1666, 'wife to three husbands'.

The three galleries, with iron piers, are original.

Above the west entrance is the mid-17C painting of 'The Last Supper' by *Francis de Cleyn*.

The chancel was rebuilt by *Teulon* in 1873, and was enlarged by the polygonal apse.

Its wooden screen was designed by *A. Blomfield* in 1898.

Mosaics behind the altar are by *Salviati*.

Outstanding wooden railings, carved by *Gibbons*, enclose the south chapel R. They were salvaged from the King's Chapel at Windsor which had been laid out for Charles II in 1682.

Displayed on the south side of the chancel's arch is the painted hatchment made for the funeral of Richard Gallis MP in 1574. He was three times mayor of Windsor and the landlord of the Garter Inn and immortalized by Shakespeare in *The Merry Wives of Windsor*. The inn stood in Thames Street but no longer survives.

Two 16C memorial tablets from the earlier church are displayed on the south wall.

In the south aisle is the monument to Catherine Grope by *T. Sharp*, 1832.

St John's possesses outstanding brasses, including some reproductions of examples from other churches in southern England. Rubbings and wax impressions may be made.

●● *Exit from the church R.*

The **Castle Hotel**, on the west side of High Street, was built early in the 19C as a posting inn.

●● *Continue ahead passing Church Lane (first R). Ahead is the Guildhall.*

Location 43	**GUILDHALL** *Fitch 1690*

High Street

Exhibition open April–September 13.30–16.30. Admission charge.

The architect *Fitch* died in 1689 and work was completed under the supervision of *Wren*. Courts sat in this building and the council held their meetings here. It was also a venue for balls.

The statue of Prince George of Denmark, consort of Queen Anne, was presented by Wren's son in 1713.

A matching eastern extension to the building R was built *c.*1830 on the site of the Shambles (street of butchers).

The Corn Exchange was once held within the arcaded open section.

It is alleged that the council insisted, against Wren's advice, that columns were needed to support the upper floor and these were duly incorporated. It can be seen, however, that they don't quite reach the ceiling.

On the north side of the Guildhall is a statue of Queen Anne, added in 1707.

•• *Enter the building and ascend the stairs to the exhibition.*

Exhibited are the borough's collection of silver plate, and regalia. Court uniforms and a description of the town's history are also displayed.

•• *Exit to High St L. First L Church Lane.*

| Location 44 | **WINDSOR'S TOWN CENTRE** |

Windsor's original town centre is a small, condensed area of five narrow streets, set in a grid pattern with ancient houses which evoke 'toy town'.

Engine House R is dated, in Roman numerals, 1803. As its name suggest, the town's fire engine was originally kept here.

The Three Tuns inn, opposite, was built in 1518 and formerly served as the Guildhall of the Holy Trinity.

On the Church Street corner (second L) **Nos 8–9** have an early 18C main facade. A Gothic shaft supporting the jetty (overhanging storey) can be seen in Church Lane which indicates that the building is probably 16C.

At the end of Church Lane R is the brick **Masonic Hall**, 1726. It was formerly a Free School and built in the style of *Wren*.

•• *Return down Church Lane. First R Church St.*

No 7, Ye Olde King's Head, 1525 (?) bears a plaque depicting the warrant for the execution of Charles I in 1649. The building was once an inn.

Nos 6 and **4, Drury House**, are late 17C. Between them, **No 5, Nell Gwyn's House**, was built in 1640. It is believed that Nell Gwyn lived here briefly.

•• *L Castle Hill. Pass Market St (first L).*

The **Horse and Groom** L was built in 1765.

•• *Return along Castle Hill. First R Market St. First R Queen Charlotte St.*

Adjoining the Guildhall L is Market Cross House.

Market Cross House is an unsupported building *c.*1718 that leans rather alarmingly northward on its timber frame.

•• *Proceed northward along High Street (towards the castle).*

Opposite, **No 24** is early 18C with a later upper storey.

No 26, The Token House, bears a plaque recording that H. G. Wells worked here as a draper's apprentice in 1880. The author would have gained much information from this experience for his book *The History of Mr Polly*.

•• *Continue to Castle Hill (R) and the* **Queen Victoria Statue.**

The statue was erected in 1887 to mark the 50th year of the Queen's reign.

•• *Ahead is Thames St. Cross the road. First L Station Approach leads to Windsor and Eton Central Station and the Royalty and Railways exhibition which is entered directly ahead.*

Location 45	**ROYALTY AND RAILWAYS EXHIBITION**

Windsor and Eton Central Station

Open daily January–March 09.30–16.30 April–December 09.30–17.30. (Closed January 20–30 for maintenance.) Admission charge.

The exhibition depicts events that took place at this station on 6 June 1897, the year of Queen Victoria's Diamond Jubilee. To mark the occasion, the station had been rebuilt by the Great Western Railway. All the waxwork models were made by Madame Tussaud's and the exhibition is accompanied by appropriate sound

Exhibited first is a full-size replica of GWR's royal train, described then as 'the finest in the world' and drawn by a Queen's Class locomotive.

Models of Queen Victoria and the Prince of Wales are seen in the royal waiting room which has been restored to its original appearance.

From a gallery, guests are viewed arriving at the station to be received by the Queen and various dignitaries, including Gladstone and Lord Salisbury. Coldstream Guards provide the guard of honour.

•• *Exit and return to Thames St L. First L Curfew Yard.*

No 2 Curfew Yard has been entirely reconstructed using much of the original 16C (?) timber.

•• *Return to Thames St L. Continue to No 18.*

Location 46	**THAMES STREET**

Nos 18–21 are early-18C houses with more recent shop fronts.

The **Theatre Royal**, founded in 1793, was rebuilt in 1910.

On the opposite side of the road, where it bends L, is the monument to Prince Christian of Schleswig Holstein, d. 1900, by *Goscombe John*. The prince, a grandson of Queen Victoria, was killed fighting for the British in the Boer War.

•• *Continue ahead.*

Old Bank House, also on the east side, was built of brick in the mid 18C as the town's bank. It is a good example of the late Palladian Revival style.

◂● Continue ahead passing the Datchet Rd junction (R).

The William the Fourth inn on the corner R was built in the early 17C.

◂● Continue ahead following Thames St.

Wren's Old House Hotel was built in 1676. It has been alleged that *Wren* designed and lived in the house.

◂● Return southward. First L Datchet Rd.

On the south side is the memorial to George V by *Lutyens*, 1936.

◂● Continue ahead, passing Windsor and Eton Riverside station.

Almost opposite, on the south side, is **St George's School** built in 1803 as a home for the Naval Knights of Windsor but now the choir school of St George's Chapel.

On the north side is the station's royal waiting room.

◂● Cross the road.

The **royal waiting room** was built by *Tite* in 1850 as part of the Southern Railway's new station. From a turret on the station an observer would look out for the arrival of the royal train. The waiting room now forms part of private offices.

The main room R possesses a bay designed in the manner of the Henry VII Chapel at Westminster Abbey.

◂● Return to Windsor and Eton Riverside Station (BR) for trains to Waterloo Station (BR).

◂● Alternatively, return to Thames St and proceed to Windsor and Eton Central Station (BR) for trains to Paddington Station (BR) (via Slough).

Eton

The Foundation Buildings of Eton College, which may be visited, form the largest complex of historic school buildings in England. Outstanding is College Chapel, most of which was completed during the lifetime of the founder, Henry VI. Further college buildings of architectural interest lie outside this complex. Eton's High Street, now an oasis of calm since the river bridge to Windsor was pedestrianized, boasts houses and inns dating from the 15C.

Timing During term time is preferable as then the ancient college precinct is open earlier. However, this is irrelevant if preceding with Windsor. The Brewhouse Gallery is only open Saturday and Sunday afternoons.

Opening details of Eton College

The precincts are generally open daily from April until the second week in October, during term 10.30–17.00; during vacations 14.00–17.00. Dates are variable. However, by booking (in writing to the custodian) other dates are available to parties of ten or more. Visitors may view School Yard, College Chapel, the Cloister, the Museum of Eton Life and the Brewhouse Gallery unaccompanied (Saturday and Sunday afternoons only). Admission charge to the precinct.

Guided Tours of Eton College
07538 63593
Guided short tours (45 minutes) take place daily 1 April–6 October at 14.15 and 15.15. These include the above, plus Lower School.

Guided extended tours (90 minutes) are as above, plus Upper School, College Hall and College grounds. Telephone for details

Guided specialist tours (two hours) are as the extended tour plus Election Hall, Election Chamber and Cloister Gallery. Telephone for details.

Groups of fifty or more must book in advance. The cost of guided tours varies according to their extent.

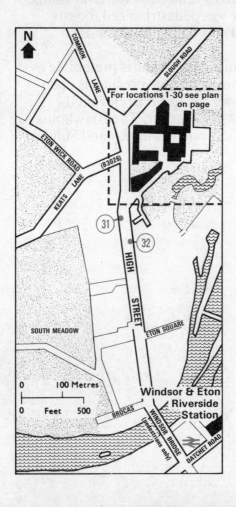

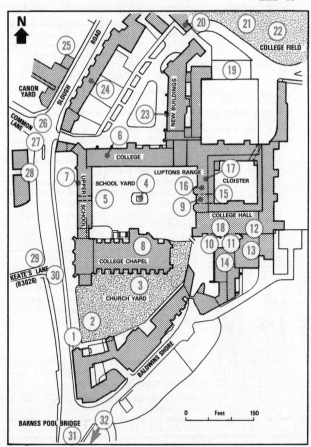

Locations

1 The Long Walk
2 Church Yard
3 College Chapel South Facade
4 Henry VI Statue
5 School Yard
6 College
7 Upper School
8 College Chapel
9 Lupton's Tower
10 Sluice Tower
11 College Hall Exterior
12 Museum of Eton Life
13 Kitchen
14 Brewhouse Gallery
15 Cloister
16 Election Chamber
17 Election Hall
18 College Hall Interior
19 King of Siam's Garden
20 Weston's
21 The Wall Game
22 College Field
23 New Buildings
24 Savile House
25 New Schools
26 Common Lane
27 The Burning Bush
28 Memorial Buildings
29 Keate's Lane
30 Slough Road
31 Barnes Pool Bridge
32 High Street

Start *Windsor and Eton Riverside Station (BR) from Waterloo Station. Exit R Datchet Rd. First R Thames St. Cross the pedestrian bridge to Eton High St. Continue to the end and cross Barnes Pool Bridge. College Chapel appears R fronted by the Long Walk pathway.*

Locations of interest south of Eton College are described on the return journey.

| Location 1 | **THE LONG WALK** |

This pathway was planted with elms in the mid 18C, but, due to disease, they have been replaced by limes. Only members of the Eton Society, known as 'Pop', may sit on the low wall which protects the path from the road.

Between the Long Walk and College Chapel is Church Yard.

| Location 2 | **CHURCH YARD** |

This is the site of Eton's parish church which was dedicated to the Assumption of the Virgin. As early as 1438 Henry VI bought the advowson (right to appoint the priest) of the church, as the initial stage in forming his college. Immediately Eton College was founded in 1440 the church was made collegiate. Services were held in the church while work on the chapel was in progress but it was demolished in 1460.

The present iron railings replaced a brick wall.

| Location 3 | **COLLEGE CHAPEL SOUTH FACADE** |

The chapel's exterior is described fully in Location 8. On the south side, the porch to the Ante Chapel was probably built *c.*1482. It served as the entrance for Eton's townspeople who by then had lost their parish church.

Immediately R of the entrance is a holy water stoup.

●● *Continue ahead. First R enter the Foundation Buildings. Proceed ahead to the Henry VI Statue in the centre of College Yard.*

●● *Alternatively, await the guide at the entrance if taking a guided tour.*

| Location 4 | **HENRY VI STATUE** *Bird 1719* |

This statue of the founder of Eton College, depicted wearing Garter robes, was donated by Provost Godolphin. Each year, on Founder's Day, 6 December, wreaths of bay leaves are laid around the statue to commemorate Henry's murder, allegedly by his usurper, Edward IV, at the Tower of London in 1471.

| Location 5 | **SCHOOL YARD** |

Henry VI originally intended that the positions of School Yard and Cloister, which lies to its east, should be transposed. When the yard was completed it was grassed over and interconnecting paths divided the area. The yard was first paved in 1707. Henry also planned that this area should be raised 10ft as a precaution against Thames floods but this was never done.

The west range, through which visitors enter, is Upper School.

The range on the north side is 'College', with Lower School occupying the western section of its ground floor and Long Chamber its entire upper floor.

Lupton's range, with its central tower through which the cloister is reached, occupies the east side.

College Chapel's north facade stretches the length of the south side.

•● Proceed to College, on the north side.

Location 6	**COLLEGE** *c.1500*

The building was free standing when completed.

Its oriel window was added in the 19C.

Open to all on guided tours. See page 52 for details.

Lower School. This was Eton's earliest recorded classroom and is probably the oldest example in the world that still serves as such.

The room is divided by double rows of pillars added, probably for structural reasons, *c.*1630.

Throughout, the woodwork, mostly 17C, is inscribed with scholars' names and initials. Robert Walpole, England's first prime minister, carved his name on the right hand shutter of the middle window in the south (entrance) wall. For long, the room was divided into three classrooms by partitions which were removed in 1917.

In the 16C, school began at 06.00 and continued until bedtime at 20.00. There were two meal breaks and a supervised leisure period of one hour. Although lessons were suspended for three weeks at Christmas, the boys were only allowed to return home for the three-week summer vacation. Greek and Latin were taught, but nothing else. The language spoken throughout the school was Latin and to speak English was a floggable offence.

Above Lower School lies Long Chamber. It is private and never open to visitors.

Long Chamber. Much of Eton's early 19C reputation for horrific bullying, torturing and sexual depravity arose from events that took place, as a matter of course, in this dormitory. It seems that at one time all seventy collegers probably slept here, generally two or three to a bed. Initially, the headmaster had his own quarters at the west end of College and the usher (later master in college) at the east end. In the 18C, however, they vacated their rooms and the boys were simply locked in the dormitory until morning, with no supervision. All hell could, and did, break loose and some of the collegers sustained grievous physical, let alone mental, injury.

In 1846, when New Buildings opened, most collegers moved there and Long Chamber was broken up into twenty-one separate cells. A further reduction to fifteen units took place in 1863 but today every colleger has his own bed-sitting room.

•● Exit R and proceed to Upper School on the west side.

Location 7	**UPPER SCHOOL** *Bankes 1694*

Open to those on guided extended and specialist tours. See page 52 for details.

An earlier building on the site had replaced the low wall which originally protected School Yard from the Slough Road. It was completed in 1670 but proved to be structurally unsafe and was demolished.

The present range of schoolrooms was allegedly designed under the supervision of *Wren*.

Its ground floor arcade links, at the south end, with the Ante Chapel of College Chapel. A Second World War bomb damaged the north end of the building which has now been restored as a replica.

Ground floor rooms were once classrooms, but, although small, up to seventy boys would be crammed into some of them. One particularly tiny room was known as the 'Black Hole'.

Headmaster's School Room. This room, seen first, was completely destroyed, along with the stairway, by the bomb. Some of the woodwork was saved, however, and was re-used. The room served as a library until converted in 1834. Since it was rebuilt, Eton's headmaster has again taught, and administered punishment, in this room.

Upper School (The Room). This was the second, and originally the largest classroom to be built at Eton. Up to two hundred boys at one time were taught here in the 18C. Slight bomb damage was faithfully restored.

The painted wall panelling has been renewed but the wainscot is original and carved with the names of numerous scholars, including the poet Shelley and politicians Fox and Gladstone.

At the north end is the headmaster's 18C desk which was restored after being splintered into fragments by the bomb.

Busts of famous Etonians line the walls.

 Exit and view the north facade of College Chapel.

Location 8	**COLLEGE CHAPEL**

Opening details as for the precincts. See page 52.

The present chapel was the second to be built on the site. Henry VI commissioned its predecessor in 1441 and Mass was celebrated there in 1443 when the walls were just a few feet high. However, in 1448, the King decided that a much grander chapel, initially a church, should be built, and the unfinished building was demolished. Henry's planned church included an aisled nave and the dimensions of the entire structure would have been similar to those of Lincoln Cathedral.

Work commenced in 1449 but proceeded slowly. It is not known who was responsible for the design of the chapel and it may have been one, or a combination of: *John Smyth*, master mason at Eton in 1448; *James Woodrofe*, a master mason who was paid for two visits in 1449, or *Robert*

Jenyns, warden of the masons in 1449.

The King provided for an establishment of forty-six, comprising priest fellows, chaplains, clerks and choristers. Many religious 'relics' were obtained, including fragments of the True Cross and the Crown of Thorns. In addition, the pope gave Eton the right, unique in England, of granting indulgences (forgiveness) to penitents. The chapel, like the parish church that preceded it, is dedicated to the Assumption of the Virgin and the privilege of granting indulgences lasted throughout the Feast that celebrated this mythical event. Many pilgrims came, prayers were said and Masses offered for the souls of Henry VI's parents, and after his death, for Henry himself.

With only the chancel completed, construction work stopped *c.* 1460 due to the Wars of the Roses and in the following year Henry was deposed by Edward IV. The chapel's relics and ornaments were then transferred, together with the members of the college, to St George's Chapel in Windsor Castle, and in spite of Eton's reprieve in 1470, much was never returned, nor was Henry's planned nave to be built. Instead, an Ante Chapel was contructed at the west end in 1482 at the expense of William of Waynflete, Bishop of Winchester and first head master (later first provost) of Eton. At the same time Waynflete founded Magdalen College, Oxford.

The entire building is 190 ft long; 40 ft shorter than St George's Chapel in Windsor Castle. If built as intended by Henry VI, it would have been twice as long again as the choir, necessitating a diversion of the Slough Road.

As a safeguard against Thames Valley floods the chapel was built on a 13 ft high base.

Teynton stone was used at the lower level, Huddlestone above this, up to the window sills, and Kentish ragstone for the upper part.

Although restored, the windows retain their original tracery pattern.

The game of Eton Fives was originally played at the foot of the stairs to the north porch, between the two buttresses.

The north porch was built in 1492 and its door is original.

Steps to this porch were rebuilt in 1695.

Immediately L of the porch is the extension added in 1515 to accommodate two subsidiary chapels. The west bay houses what is now the Memorial Chapel and the east bay Lupton's Chapel.

The Ante Chapel at the west end of College Chapel is slightly lower, and north and south wings give it the appearance of a transept.

Its walls were refaced with Bath stone in 1876.

•➡ Enter College Chapel via its Ante Chapel which is reached from the door beneath the west end of Upper School's arcade.

This door is *c.*1482.

The **Ante Chapel** was used for worship by Eton's parishioners, but the choir of the chapel was always reserved for the college.

Immediately L is the painting 'Sir Galahad' by *Watts*, a copy by the artist of his original work.

Dividing the Ante Chapel from the choir is the screen by *Street*, 1882. Before this was built there was no separation.

The organ case above was designed by *Pearson* in 1871.

Brasses on the walls, were originally fixed in the floor of the choir.

In the centre, against the west wall, is the statue of Henry VI depicted holding a model of the chapel by *Bacon*, 1784.

The tester of the 18C pulpit has been converted to a table top and stands R of the screen.

●● *Enter the choir.*

Choir. Only boys in their last two years at Eton attend services in this chapel as it is too small to accommodate the entire school.

Dominating the choir is the vaulted ceiling designed by *Sir William Holford* in 1959. It imitates late Tudor fan vaults but is in fact composed of stone-faced, lightweight concrete panels suspended from steel trusses. The chief apparent difference between this and genuine Tudor fan vaulting is that the panels are not decoratively shaped, e.g. there are no cusps or diamond patterns.

Henry VI may have originally intended that the chapel should be vaulted with stone and the presence of external buttresses to withstand a heavy downward and outward thrust indicates that he did. In the event, a timber ceiling was installed for Waynflete *c.*1479. This was renewed in 1699 but became unsafe due to infestation by death watch beetles and was replaced by the present vault. Holford's work was, therefore, the first stone vault to be built in the chapel choir's five hundred years of existence.

College Chapel's most important possession is the set of rare grisaille (grey monochrome) wall paintings executed between 1479 and 1488 on the first four bays of the choir's north and south walls. They have been judged the most important large scale 15C paintings to survive in northern Europe. Each scene is separated from its neighbour by *trompe-l'oeil* columns, with niches in which statues of saints are placed. It is believed that the prime object of the paintings, which increase the apparent width of the nave, was to divide the chapel visually into a chancel and an aisled nave, once it became clear that Henry's projected nave would never be built. The rood screen, which stood at a point just past where the paintings now terminate, would have contributed towards this effect.

All the paintings had been whitewashed over by the college barber in 1560, following the Reformation. Wainscoting, added in the early 18C, concealed them further but in 1847 this was stripped off so that new canopied stalls could be fixed to the walls. The paintings were then revealed, but unfortunately workmen removed most of the upper row on both walls and were only stopped from completing their destruction by the timely arrival of a member of the college. Nevertheless, the canopies were fitted over what remained and it was not until 1923 that the paintings were revealed again when these were removed. All that survived has now been carefully restored.

At least four master painters, with their assistants, were probably involved in the work. Only two are recorded, *William Baker*, for the last year only, and *Gilbert*.

Scenes on the north wall illustrate miracles of the Virgin Mary. Latin captions describe each scene.

➤ Proceed to the south wall.

Paintings on the south wall tell the tale of an empress falsely accused; a story related by Chaucer, amongst others.

➤ Return to the north wall and proceed eastward.

At the east end of the north choir stalls is the brass lectern *c.*1501, originally a music stand.

The first door in the wall leads to the north porch.

War Memorial Chapel. Together with the adjacent Lupton's Chapel, this was built *c.*1515. It had served as the vestry until its conversion in 1922 to commemorate Etonians who had been killed in the First World War. Almost two thousand Old Etonians died in the two World Wars.

➤ Proceed to the next bay.

Lupton's Chapel. This was built as a chantry chapel for Provost Roger Lupton.

Lupton's rebus an R and LUP on a tun (barrel), is carved on the screen which is original.

The intricate design of the chapel's Tudor fan vault contrasts with the plainness of the choir's modern 'fan vault'.

'Presentation in the Temple', painted by *West*, is on the wall R.

➤ Continue ahead.

Stained glass windows on the north and south walls at the east end of the choir are by *John Piper*.

Within the sanctuary, against the north wall, is the tomb of Provost Murray, d.1535, by *Maximilian Colt*. It is the largest monument in the chapel.

Stained glass in the east window was designed by *Evie Home* and inserted in 1952.

The arch of the east window changes from a steep to a less steep form, probably indicating that work at this end stopped temporarily during the troubled period between 1460 and 1470.

Below the windows are tapestries woven at Merton Abbey in 1895 to designs by *Burne-Jones*. The central tapestry depicts the Adoration. This was hung on the south wall until moved to its present position in 1905.

Both side panels were adapted from the same designer's work at Salisbury Cathedral.

•● *Exit from College Chapel and proceed towards Lupton's Tower in the centre of the east range of School Yard.*

Location 9	**LUPTON'S TOWER**

The tower was built for Provost Roger Lupton by *Henry Redman* c.1520. It stands in the centre of the east range of School Yard, which is known as Lupton's range.

The base of the double oriel window above the gateway is decorated with two angels holding a heraldic shield.

Above the lower window is a medallion depicting the Assumption of the Virgin.

On the north turret L, black bricks on the third stage are set to represent a vase of Annunciation lilies.

Above the clock face are the arms of Henry VIII.

The lead cupolas surmounting the turrets were added in 1765 to house the bells when the clock was transferred here from the east end of College Chapel's north wall.

Little is known about the building history of the sections, on either side of the gateway, that make up Lupton's range. It is generally accepted that an earlier range, probably completed c.1460, stood here and that this was partly remodelled or rebuilt by Lupton c.1520. Their interiors are described later when the cloister (Location 15) is reached.

•● *Proceed to the south-east corner of School Yard. Continue through the arch to Brewhouse Yard. Turn L and pass the south end of Lupton's range. Attached to this R is the sluice tower.*

Location 10	**SLUICE TOWER**

Built partly of stone and partly of brick, this short tower once regulated the flow of water into the sewers.

•● *Proceed to the adjoining College Hall.*

Location 11	**COLLEGE HALL EXTERIOR**

The hall was in use, primarily for dining purposes, by 1450, probably in an unfinished state because, as can be seen, the stonework ends at the upper level and the building was completed in brick, much of which was restored in the 18C.

The interior of College Hall is described later.

At the far end of the hall is the entrance L to the Museum of Eton Life.

| Location 12 | **MUSEUM OF ETON LIFE** |

Opening details as for the precincts. See page 52.

This recently opened museum on the lower floor of College Hall describes the history of Eton from its conception to the present day.

Boys' rooms at Eton during various periods have been reconstructed.

The birch and birching block used by Eton's longest serving headmaster, Dr Keate (1809–34) are exhibited. Keate was feared for his beatings which occasionally appeared to be sadistic, however, his task in controlling so many boys was a difficult one. Dr Keate was the last headmaster to teach all the senior boys, up to two hundred, in Upper School at the same time. He was a gifted orator and two of his pupils, later to become prime ministers, Lord Derby and Gladstone, must have learnt much from him.

•• *Exit from the museum to the kitchen at the south-east end of the hall.*

| Location 13 | **KITCHEN** |

Although much restored, the kitchen was built in 1507 and part of its ancient core remains (best viewed from the rear of Brewhouse Yard). It still serves as one of Eton's kitchens.

•• *Return westward passing L the Brewhouse Gallery which faces College Hall.*

| Location 14 | **BREWHOUSE GALLERY** *1714* |

Open Saturday and Sunday 14.30–17.00. See page 52 for details.

Recently converted to an art gallery, the Brewhouse was built for the brewing of Eton College Audit Ale. Hops were obtained from the hop garden owned by the college in Common Lane and brewing continued here until 1869. It was customary in the 18C for boys to consume alcoholic drinks.

Paintings relating to the history of Eton and Etonians are displayed, including some 'leavers'. These were paintings of themselves presented by Etonians to the headmaster when they left the college. In the mid 18C it was customary for a boy to give money (£15 or £30), the amount depending on the status of his family. In return, the headmaster presented the scholar with an inscribed book, usually the collected poems of Gray, who was himself an Etonian. Now, it is customary for boys to give their photograph to masters and friends when they leave.

Some works exhibited feature Etonians in exotic costumes celebrating Montem, a custom which lasted from the 16C to the 19C. The entire school marched, as a regiment, from School Yard 'ad montem' (to the hill) south of Slough, accompanied by a military band. Salt bearers and twelve servitors in particularly colourful dress collected money along the route. George III and

Queen Charlotte were particularly fond of this ceremony which then took place triennially; each gave fifty guineas and attended whenever possible. All proceeds were given to the school captain to meet the day's expenses and support him later at university. Montem ended in 1844, much to the regret of Queen Victoria, because the new railway to Slough brought unmanageable crowds.

Some Montem costumes are also displayed.

Return to School Yard. Turn R and proceed through Lupton's Tower to the cloister.

Location 15	**CLOISTER**

The cloister is the oldest part of Eton College and it was here that all members of the Foundation, including the original twenty-four scholars, had their lodgings.

The north and east ranges (L and ahead) are believed to have been built between 1443 and 1448. They are of brick, a rare building material for this period, rather than stone.

The second storey, with an attic, was added to both ranges by *Leadbetter* in 1758 and much remodelling has since taken place.

The protective railings, of Sussex iron, were made in 1725.

Turn L and proceed clockwise around the cloister to the east side ahead. From here may be viewed the south and west ranges, separated by Lupton's Tower.

It is probable that an earlier range on the south side matched the remainder of the cloister before the present block was erected in the Classical style. This was designed, specifically to house the library, by the clerk of works at Windsor Castle, *Thomas Rowland*, in 1773. It possesses the finest Classical rooms at Eton but these are, unfortunately, no longer open to the public. Amongst many rare books in Eton's collection is a Gutenberg Bible *c.*1455.

Behind the library is the south facade of College Hall which was remodelled when the library was built.

The large buttress against Lupton's Tower, was added in 1910 as there were indications of structural problems.

The west range, R of Lupton's Tower R, was rebuilt, or remodelled, at the same time as the tower was constructed *c.*1570.

Its north-east stair turret was enlarged in 1618.

On the first floor of Lupton's Tower is Election Chamber.

Location 16	**ELECTION CHAMBER**

Open to those on guided specialist tours. See page 52 for details.

In this room boys were once elected (after examination) as collegers and later as undergraduates at King's College, Cambridge.

The panelling is late 17C.

Immediately north of this chamber, in the west range of the cloister, is Election Hall.

| Location 17 | **ELECTION HALL** |

Open to those on guided specialist tours. See page 52 for details.

Lupton created this room *c.*1520 to house the library, which it did until the present library was built. The hall then became the chamber where scholars awaited their examination in Election Chamber.

The outstanding Tudor screen at the north end was made *c.*1549.

Some 16C stained glass cartouches survive in the windows.

Against the east wall is a long table on which shovelboard was played. Prince Albert's skill, demonstrated on this table, was described as 'adroit'.

Adjoining Election Hall are the lodgings of the provost. The vice-provost and headmaster also live in the cloister but the fellows now reside outside college premises.

| Location 18 | **COLLEGE HALL INTERIOR** |

Open to those on guided extended and specialist tours. See page 52 for details.

When completed *c.*1520, the fellows, headmaster, collegers and commensals all dined in this hall twice daily. Friday, however, was a day of fasting and no meals were provided. Oppidans, who replaced commensals after the Restoration, never dined in College Hall. Collegers still take their meals here.

The appearance of the hall's interior owes much to the restoration of 1858. At this time, the roof was rebuilt, the west window remodelled, the screen made and some of the panelling of 1547 replaced.

During this restoration, the original Tudor fireplaces were discovered. They had never been used, however, because no chimneys existed; another demonstration of last minute economy. As in most halls of that period, a central fire burned and its smoke escaped through a louvre in the roof.

Leave the cloister from the north-east corner.

The range of buildings L, in Tudor style, extends northward from the Provost's Lodge in Lupton's range. It was built in 1765.

Continue ahead and turn L to the King of Siam's Garden.

| Location 19 | **KING OF SIAM'S GARDEN** |

This garden was laid out in 1929 at the expense of Old Etonian King Prajadhipok of Siam (now Thailand) following a visit to Eton after his abdication. It was previously the site of the Provosts Stables, later used as a garage.

The statue of Perseus holding the Gorgon's head is by *Lajos Strobl.*

Follow the path L to Weston's.

Location 20	**WESTON'S**

The 18C front conceals an earlier house, built in 1678. It was constructed partly on the site of the original college almshouse which survived until 1468.

John Newborough, later headmaster, is known to have lived here and some boys boarded in the house. It is named after Stephen Weston, an early-18C master who became Bishop of Exeter.

North of Weston's can be seen the long wall against which the Eton Wall Game is played.

Location 21	**THE WALL GAME**

This game, incomprehensible to outsiders, is played annually on St Andrew's Day, between ten collegers and ten oppidans. It was originally called 'Shirking Walls' and began soon after the wall was built in 1717. One goal is the stump of an elm tree, known as Bad Calx, the opposite goal is the garden door to Weston's known as Good Calx.

In front of the wall is College Field.

Location 22	**COLLEGE FIELD**

College Field is protected from the Slough Road by 'the wall' and forms part of Eton's extensive playing fields. Henry VI acquired land so that the boys could practise archery, but in the 18C at least twenty-three games were played at Eton; few of them now exist. The Duke of Wellington was one of Eton's most famous scholars. However, there is no record of his actually saying 'The battle of Waterloo was won on the playing fields of Eton' even though they were probably his sentiments. It was on College Field that the six-day fair was held between c.1450 and 1460 to cater for pilgrims seeking indulgences during the Feast of the Assumption.

•● Continue ahead and proceed through Weston's Yard. New Buildings is the long range L which is preceded by the college sick rooms.

Location 23	**NEW BUILDINGS** *J. Shaw 1846*

The construction of this block spelt the demise of the miserable conditions in the Long Chamber dormitory. For the first time, collegers were provided with individual rooms, like oppidans in their boarding houses. Provost Hodgson was responsible for this great reform. 'Please God I will do something for these poor boys' he is reported to have said on his first day at Eton. Prince Albert laid the foundation stone in 1844 but forgot to remove his kid gloves which were ruined by the wet mortar. 'There goes three and six (18p) and serve him right' Etonians are recorded as saying; Prince Albert had not yet become a popular figure.

On the opposite side of Weston's Yard is an 18C house, originally the headmaster's residence.

•● Continue ahead, passing R Savile House.

Location 24	**SAVILE HOUSE**

Built early in the 17C, Savile House was badly damaged by a bomb in the Second World War; miraculously none were killed. Originally, the house had been commissioned by Provost Savile to accommodate the college's printing press.

The section fronting Weston's Yard was completely rebuilt and now provides houses for the masters (beaks).

External Jacobean features survive at the rear, facing Slough Road.

•● *Continue to Slough Rd R. Immediately opposite is New Schools.*

The complex known as The Foundation Buildings has now been left but many college properties of historic and architectural interest lie outside this.

Location 25	**NEW SCHOOLS** *Woodyer 1863*

These buildings, which provided greatly needed new classroom accommodation, were commissioned by Dr Hawtrey, a reforming headmaster. They occupy part of the old Hop Garden where hops had been grown in the 18C for ale, brewed in the Brew House.

Opposite are the Jacobean rear facades of Savile House that survived the bomb damage.

•● *Return southward. First R Common Lane. Immediately R fronting New Schools is Cannon Yard.*

Location 26	**COMMON LANE**

Cannon Yard was named from the gun which was presented to the college and stands in the yard. It had been captured at Sebastapol during the Crimean War in 1867.

Immediately opposite is Manor House.

Manor House. The Duke of Wellington boarded here under the care of its dame, Miss Naylor.

A top storey, south wing and bay were additons to this late-18C house.

•● *Continue ahead. Immediately opposite is the 18C* **Common Lane House**.

•● *Bear L. Immediately L is Godolphin House.*

Godolphin House was built by headmaster Dr Snape (1711–20). Its name, however, commemorates Dr Godolphin who was provost at the time.

•● *Ahead is Holland House.*

Holland House. Dr Keate was the master in charge of this boarding house before he was appointed headmaster. It has mostly been rebuilt.

•● *Return to Common Lane L. Cross the road and follow the short drive to Angelo's.*

Angelo's was built *c*.1790 but has since been extended. Its name commemorates Miss Angelo, a well-known early-19C dame.

•● Return to Slough Rd R. Immediately R is the 'Burning Bush' lamp-post.

Location 27	**THE BURNING BUSH**

This cast-iron lamp-post was made in 1864, but stood in the centre of the road until 1963. It soon became a famous Eton landmark and gained the name Burning Bush because of its extravagant design.

The two buildings R form Memorial Buildings.

Location 28	**MEMORIAL BUILDINGS** *L. K. Hall 1908*

Built in Baroque style, to commemorate Etonians who had died in the Boer War, are the domed library R and the hall L.

The hall was designed to accommodate the entire school (then 1200) but fire regulations no longer permit this number to congregate within. It stands on the site of Mrs Hatton's early-19C lolly-pop shop. This was known as 'Pop' and it was here that the Eton Society held its debates when it was founded in 1811. The society is still known as 'Pop' but activities are now mainly sporting. Members, who wear fancy waistcoats and check trousers, are responsible for college discipline.

•● Continue ahead. First R Keate's Lane (signposted B3026 Maidenhead).

Location 29	**KEATE'S LANE**

The name of this lane, of course, commemorates Eton's longest serving headmaster, Dr Keate. It had previously been called Goodall Lane in honour of his predecessor.

Carter House, on the corner L, was built in the 17C. Its upper storey was added later. Both Thomas and his son William Carter, who taught at Eton, lived in the house and later became fellows.

A plaque on the wall indicates the point where Henry VI's chapel was designed to reach.

Ballards, on the opposite side, commemorates a Lord of the Manor of Eton. It was built in the 18C but the doorcase, in the style of *Kent*, was brought from elsewhere.

Evans's, opposite, commemorates Jane Evans, Eton's last dame, who died in 1906. It was built as a wash-house in the 18C before being converted to boarding accommodation by Jane's father, William.

On the corner R is **Keate House** built *c*.1785. It was the residence of Dr Keate from 1809 to 1834. Following Keate's retirement it became a boarding house.

•● Return to Slough Rd R.

Passed immediately R is the main facade of Carter House.

| Location 30 | **SLOUGH ROAD** |

Old St Christophers (1 and 2 Hodgson House). This early Georgian house was originally the Christopher inn established in the 16C. It became a boarding house *c.*1840 when the college acquired the property.

St Christopher's is an early 19C boarding house.

•● The first path R is signposted to Gullivers.

Immediately L is **Gullivers**, once a boarding house but now residences for masters. Its front, in effect several properties, is early 18C but the half-timbered rear, passed later, betrays its older history, possibly early 17C.

Jourdelays, at the end of the lane R, was rebuilt by headmaster Dr Snape *c.*1720. It was originally two and a half storeys high and, together with Godolphin House, was the first boarding house at Eton to be built as such. Thomas Jourdelay was a 15C owner of an earlier house that stood on the site.

•● Return to Slough Rd R.

Immediately R is the half-timbered rear of Gullivers.

On the corner opposite, is the brick-built **Corner House.** Gladstone lodged at the Corner House in 1821 but that house was rebuilt shortly afterwards.

Baldwins Shore, actually on the corner, is the first house in the street of that name which commemorates an open sewer that once ran here. It was believed to be a source of malaria.

The house was rebuilt as a replica in the 1960s, re-using its 17C roof tiles.

•● Continue ahead to Barnes Pool Bridge.

| Location 31 | **BARNES POOL BRIDGE** |

In the 15C this was known as Baldwyne Brigge and its upkeep has always been paid for by an ancient trust. The present structure was erected in 1884.

A stone on Bridge House R indicates the flood levels of 1894 and 1947.

The boundaries of Eton College have now been left. Until 1860 the High Street, that begins here, was 'out of bounds' to the college boys. To overcome this it was customary for boys to dart into a shop if a master, or sixth former appeared. This was known as 'shirking' and was tacitly permitted.

| Location 32 | **HIGH STREET** |

Properties in the street date from 1420 but the majority are Georgian. Since the bridge across the Thames was pedestrianized, Eton's High Street has regained much of its ancient calm as through traffic has been eliminated.

Early 19C houses line the first part of the west

side but properties of greatest interest commence at No 17 on the east side. Street numbering is unusual in that it proceeds southward along the east side and continues northward along the west side. The following houses are all on the east side.

No 17 is 18C.

Nos 22–8 are early 19C.

No 29 bears a wall plaque explaining that it was built in 1812 as a parish school.

Nos 38–40 are early 18C.

No 42 was built *c*.1787 as two houses. The bay is later.

➤ *First L Eton Square.*

On the opposite side of the road are the **College Almshouses,** built for elderly ladies by Provost Godolphin in 1714.

➤ *Return to High St L and cross the road.*

Turks Head Antiques, built *c*.1500, was a tavern until 1950. Its carved demons, flanking the arch and windows, came from elsewhere and are probably continental.

Opposite, just before the Cockpit Restaurant, is a rare early Victorian pillar box.

The Cockpit Restaurant, Eton's oldest house, was built in 1420. Cock fighting took place here in the 17C, reputedly patronized by Charles II. The building was never an inn.

Stocks exhibited outside the restaurant were used at Eton in the 18C. Wrongdoers were trapped in them for various lengths of time and, if unpopular, would be pelted with rotten fruit and eggs.

No 90, on the west side, is early 18C.

No 87 is late 17C.

The **Crown and Cushion** inn was built in the 17C.

➤ *Cross the pedestrian* **Windsor Bridge.**

This iron bridge replaced a timber structure in 1833. It was recently pedestrianized.

➤ *Ahead Thames St. First L Datchet Rd and Windsor and Eton Riverside Station (BR) to Waterloo Station.*

➤ *Alternatively, follow Thames St to Station Aproach and Windsor and Eton Central Station (BR) to Paddington Station via Slough.*

England's rulers and major events at Windsor Castle

	House of Normandy	
1066	*William I,* *'The Conqueror'* Matilda of Flanders	First construction work at Windsor of a motte, wooden buildings and ditch *c.*1070
1087	*William II 'Rufus'*	
1100	*Henry I* Matilda Adelicia	First Court held at Windsor; the King occupies apartments, probably timber built, 1110
1135	*Stephen* Matilda	
	House of Plantagenet	
1154	*Henry II* Eleanor of Aquitaine	Walls, except on south side, bastion towers, keep (Round Tower) and royal apartments rebuilt of stone 1165–71 Formal state buildings erected in Lower Ward 1171
1189	*Richard I 'Coeur de Lion'* Berengaria of Navarre	Rebellious brother of the King, the future King John, besieged in the castle for one month in 1194
1199	*John* Avisa Isabella	John again besieged in the castle for three months in 1215
1216	*Henry III* Eleanor	South Wall and bastion towers of Lower Ward built 1220–6 Fire destroyed most royal apartments in Lower Ward – the Great Hall survived – 1226 Deans Cloister built 1240 The castle's first chapel completed 1248 Royal apartments in Upper Ward rebuilt 1250
1272	*Edward I* Eleanor of Castile Margaret	
1307	*Edward II* Isabella	Future Edward III born at the castle 1313
1327	*Edward III* Phillippa of Hainault	King David II of Scotland imprisoned in the Round Tower 1346 Order of the Garter founded *c.*1348 Royal apartments rebuilt and extended on the north side of the Upper Ward *c.*1350 Chapel converted for the Garter ceremonies 1354 Deanery built as a chapter house for Knights of the Garter 1354 Norman Gateway built 1355 Canon's Cloister built 1356 King Jean of France imprisoned in the Round Tower 1356 Belfry for the chapel built (now the Mary Tudor Tower) *c.*1359

1377	*Richard II* Anne of Bohemia	
1399	**House of Lancaster** *Henry IV* Mary Joanna	
1413	*Henry V* Catherine of Valois	King James I of Scotland imprisoned in the Round Tower 1413–24 Chapter Library built, probably as a hall for the priest vicars and clerks 1415
1422	*Henry VI* Margaret of Anjou	Henry VI born at Windsor 1421
1461	**House of York** *Edward IV* Elizabeth	Construction of St George's Chapel commenced 1475 Curfew Tower converted to form bell tower of St George's Chapel 1477 Horseshoe Cloister built as houses for priest vicars 1481
1483	*Edward V*	
1483	*Richard III* Anne of Warwick	Garter ceremony transferred to the uncompleted St George's Chapel 1483 Body of Henry VI transferred from Chertsey Abbey to St George's Chapel *c.*1484
1485	**House of Tudor** *Henry VII* Elizabeth of York	Construction of St George's Chapel continued. Original chapel adapted as a proposed tomb house for Henry VI and Henry VII 1494 Royal Apartments extended westward by the construction of the Henry VII Building
1509	*Henry VIII* Catherine of Aragon Anne Boleyn Jane Seymour Anne of Cleves Catherine Howard Catherine Parr	Henry VIII Gateway built 1511 West front of St George's Chapel completed 1511 Thomas Wolsey acquired the earlier chapel 1514 Interior of St George's Chapel completed 1528 North Terrace built (of timber) 1533
1547	*Edward VI*	
1553	*Lady Jane Grey* Lord Dudley	
1553	*Mary I* Philip II of Spain	New accommodation completed for the Poor Knights 1558 Original Queen's Beasts added to St Georges Chapel 1557
1558	*Elizabeth I*	North Terrace rebuilt of stone 1578 Queen Elizabeth's Gallery built 1583
1603	**House of Stuart** *James I* Anne of Denmark	
1625	*Charles I* Henrietta Maria	Parliamentary forces seized the castle 1642

	Commonwealth	
	1649–60	
1660	*Charles II*	Royal apartments rebuilt by *May*
	Catherine of Braganza	1670–75
		Queen's Tower built by *May* 1680
1685	*James II*	
	Anne Hyde	
	Mary of Modena	
1689	*William III*	Priest vicars hall converted to
	and Mary II	accommodate Chapter Library 1694
	(joint rulers)	
1702	*Anne*	
	George of Denmark	
	House of Hanover	
1714	*George I*	
	Sophia Dorothea	
1727	*George II*	
	Caroline of Anspach	
1760	*George III*	Most windows rebuilt in Gothic style by
	Charlotte	*Wyatt* 1804
		George III died at Windsor 1820
1820	*George IV*	Royal apartments converted to State
	Caroline of Brunswick	Apartments, new royal apartments
		constructed, Round Tower doubled in
		height, walls restored, bastion towers
		rebuilt and St George's Gate built. All
		by *Wyatville* 1820–27
		George IV died at Windsor 1830
1830	*William IV*	Poor Knights renamed Military Knights
	Adelaide	1833
		Queen Elizabeth's Gallery and the
		Henry VII Building converted to house
		the royal library 1834
		William IV died at Windsor 1837
1837	*Victoria*	Windsor Castle, Victoria's favourite
	Albert	residence, became the social centre of
		the country
		Royal Mews built by *Blore* 1842
		Henry II's Great Hall in Lower Ward
		demolished 1859
		Albert, the Prince Consort, dies of
		typhoid at the castle 1861
		Guard Room built by *Salvin* 1862
		Future Edward VII married in
		St George's Chapel 1863
		Curfew Tower remodelled by *Salvin*
		1863
		Grand Staircase to State Apartments
		constructed by *Salvin* 1866
		Western approach added to
		St George's Chapel by *George Gilbert*
		Scott 1870
		Royal Mausoleum at Frogmore
		completed 1871
		Old Chapel remodelled internally and
		renamed the Albert Memorial Chapel
		1873
		St George's Chapel heavily restored by
		Pearson 1886

	House of Saxe Coburg	
1901	*Edward VII* Alexandra	
	House of Windsor	
1910	*George V* Mary of Teck	Doll's House presented by the nation to Queen Mary 1923. Now displayed at the castle South porch of St George's Chapel built 1926
1936	*Edward VIII* *(later Duke of Windsor)*	
1936	*George VI* Elizabeth Bowes-Lyon	
1952	*Elizabeth II* Philip	Prince Harry baptised in St Georges Chapel 1985